NO

TIME

TO

KILL

Timothy Knecht

No Time to Kill

In memory of

Sarah Podlin 1984-2002

Sean Berkley 1984-2005

Mary Knecht 1935-2012

Gone but never forgotten

Dossier of Missions

The City Different

Most of you do not know me, but my name is Joseph Scapeotto. Everybody calls me Joey. I am the best CIA officer in America. When I was six my parents were murdered in cold blood, point blank range, right in front of me. We were leaving a carnival when it happened and I will never forget that day or the man who shot my parents. I had just got into the car when they were shot and for an unknown reason my life was spared. Borishkov Medea, a member of the early Russian KGB, killed my parents. My father was also a CIA officer though I always remember my father telling me that he was a contractor for the Army Peace Corps. I guess that was what he told mom and me as a cover story so we would not know he worked for the Agency.

I joined the CIA after being a sharpshooter for the Army Special Forces in Vietnam. I left the war and started teaching at the Baltimore police academy. I became a control tactics and SWAT instructor. I got the job because I was one of the top five snipers in the country. After a year of teaching for the Baltimore PD I was recruited by the CIA. It did not hurt that I taught myself to speak perfect and fluent Russian and German.

My problems got started one month ago when I paid the Italian Mafia ten thousand dollars to help me capture Michael Balepta. Balepta is a bloodthirsty assassin the CIA wanted captured. The mafia, for once, was willing to take a job outside their interests. They were willing to capture Balepta if I was willing to pay a contribution to the family. My contribution was ten thousand dollars, which is a little less than what the government actually gave me for expenses on this case. When you cannot find the man you are looking for and someone else is willing to turn him over, of course you are going to pay any price to capture that man. If you were in my situation, I think you would have done the same thing. It surprised me big time to see the Italian mafia help out a lawman. There help must have been because of my cover story that I was a hit man looking for Balepta. When your cousin is an accountant for one of the mafia bosses and he vouches for you, I guess they cut you a little slack. From this day on I have never had any problems with the Italian mafia in the New York City region. I think you can see why.

Since I obtained the services of the mafia, most everyone at the CIA distrusts me. Half think of me as a traitor for working with the mafia and the rest distrust me for doing so. I do not blame them, would you? To prove my loyalty the CIA powers that be sent me to Santa Fe, New Mexico so that I can follow up on a lead about one of America's most wanted KGB officers, Madam Anna Layata. I was never a traitor or prosecuted as one even though some would have liked to see me in court for my actions. For my punishment they sent me to do a rookie's job. To this very day I am still baffled at how we let a wanted KGB agent slip right on to our own soil. To make things worse nobody would tell me anything about how she got to Santa Fe except that I might be able to find clues about her plans there. You would think that someone would have enlightened me on this enquiry, but instead I just got a plane ticket and some new gear from the tech boys downstairs.

Madam Anna Layata is a KGB officer, assassin, and a leader of her own six to eight person spy team. I am to this day baffled of how she came to be a team leader. Anna is a slim woman who has a swimsuit model an athletically toned body that turns most heads. Her light auburn hair lies just longer than her shoulders. Her hazel eyes can bring most men to do anything she wants. She loves seducing others with her full rose colored lips. The rest of her face reminds one of a young Brooke Shields and she stands three inches short of six feet tall. The GRU is Russia's foreign military intelligence agency while the KGB is the intelligence agency for almost everything else. Madam Layata is also a trained GRU Spetsnaz or Russian Special Forces agent. She was born in a small village located south west of Petrozavodsk in the same year as Israeli independence. Her village lies between Lake Ladoga and Lake Onega. The closest major city to her village that you would know is Leningrad, which is now known as St. Petersburg. The actual name of her village is unknown to the CIA, but we do know that she was recruited by the GRU at the young age of between seven and ten. She spent her childhood training to be a GRU officer.

In her early twenties Madam Layata was caught in the then United Kingdom territory of Hong Kong and was turned over to US military officers to be tried by the courts of USA. In 1971 she was going to be tried in for the late 1960's killing three US delegates to the North-South Vietnamese border, supplying Vietcong with weapons, and the attack on the US embassy in Seoul, Korea where several high ranking American officers were brutally killed. Two of Madam Layata's fellow group members were arrested in connection with the 1967 riots in Hong Kong that filled the streets with thousands of homemade bombs. Authorities believed she was involved with the riots, but the evidence against her was circumstantial. The military officers that Madam Layata was turned over to happened to be undercover KGB operatives that smuggled her out of Hong Kong and into China where she was undetected and silent for a few years. When she resurfaced she was the leader of her own spy team.

I got to Santa Fe at fourteen hundred hours on the twelfth of March nineteen eighty two. Even though the CIA mandate states that an operative shall not work in the USA, I was told to go the New Mexico and reminded that if I was caught I was to be on my own with no agency help. It was a mildly hot spring day, and as I got to my hotel I noticed some strange short male in a blue overcoat with cut up jeans was watching me and had followed me from the airport. When you have been working for the CIA as long as I have, eight years to this day, it is easy to spot these kinds of things. His glasses were thick and red. His green hat covered his semi-long brown hair. After a couple of minutes of observing the man I went inside. Never thought I would see an old hefty man half nude behind the counter, but there he was with a fat cigar in his mouth. The lobby was small and crammed full of people and it smelled like rotten eggs in the stale air. A couple of hours after I got settled in and napped, I took a walk around the city to see if I could find information about the whereabouts of Madam Layata.

Some of the locals told me that there was an archaeological dig located forty minutes north of the city. I was told that some stupid horse riders found a very old burial site with several bones and artifacts. Most of the people that I talked to believed that it was a government cover up and the real thing that was found was nuclear materials left over and buried in the desert after the end of the Manhattan Project. The latter explanation makes sense why Madam Layata would be in Santa Fe. There is nothing the Russians would not do to get the upper hand in the nuclear arms race.

After talking to some of the locals I arrived in an abandoned neighborhood. Supposedly a feud between Mexican and Chinese gangs ran the neighborhood into a ghetto and the locals packed up and left it to the gangs to fight it out. A short feud ensued because the state troops along with FBI gang taskforces ran the thugs out of town and since then nobody come back. I figured it would be a good part of town for a couple of spies to hide out in. Who would want to look for somebody in a nasty abandoned and rundown neighborhood? I bet some of you would look there out of curiosity. I did it out of instinct.

When I got down to First and Alpine Street, located on the outer portion of town, I came to the weird conclusion that I was not alone. You might call this feeling my gut but I call it an acquired skill. As I turned around I caught a glimpse of four men jumping into an alley. It was the kind of eerie, garbage filled, and smelly alley you would not want to be seen in after dark. The men were average build. I thought it was nothing and kept on walking. Nearby there was a peculiar smell in the air. The smell was like a cherry blossom turnover. That was the smell of Madam Layata's trademark perfume. It's a smell you cannot miss. This was a sure sign that Madam Layata was here not too long ago.

I knew something was going to happen, but what I could not say. I do not even think you could have told me what was going to happen. Bang! Bang! I heard the shots ring up and down the street. I turned the corner of Albine Street and took off over the chain link fence. I scaled that fence faster than a marine climbing the wall at the obstacle course. Without thinking, I dove over the garbage cans on my left and then fired six shots from my M1911A1 .45 automatic handgun. I killed the first two gunman but the two others got lucky.

When I came back to reality and came to my senses, I realized that the probability of me getting out of this situation alive was very slim. The way I saw things was that if I have to die the last two gunmen are going with me. Looking around I noticed that I was near an abandoned gas station. It was an Amoco station and much to my surprise the station had a couple of full barrels of crude oil on its lot.

Out of my pocket I took a small container of C4 explosive putty and stuck it on top of a container of crude oil. The explosive putty is the same size as a pack of gum and lucky for me that it never exploded in my coat pocket. I ran into the building across the street, a small sized dance hall. I am not sure why the dance hall doors were open and why the hall was empty. It just was that way. Next to the dance hall is an abandoned building that used to be used as private cooking school until unsanitary conditions shut it down. Why anyone would build a dance hall near a gas station is beyond me. Anyway, after I entered the dance hall, I turned and shot the oil container, which exploded on contact.

Looking through the nearest window, I noticed the explosion created a decent-sized hole in the ground along with filling the air with smoke, metal shrapnel from the containers, and the smell of burning flesh. I felt sorry for the two gunmen and I think you would agree with me. The blast of the oil combined with the intense heat disintegrated the skin off the gunmen's face, leaving their skulls and bodies partially skinless and lifeless.

The dance hall was not huge but it was not small either. Hanging from the center of the hall was the biggest chandelier I have ever seen. Any one of you would have agreed with me. It had to be the size of an average car. In the center of the room was three tables. The two end tables each had only two lit candles on each edge. The middle table had only two candles, just like the other two tables, with the addition of a cooking pot with a huge lid for a crock-pot on top of it. Why was it there? I do not know and it really does not matter. As curious as I am, like most of you, I took the lid off the pot to see why it was there and noticed that I had started a timer on a bomb. We all have our stupid moments and this was one of mine. I had twenty seconds to leave the building or become dead like a rabbit in a fight with a lion. I headed back out the same way I came in. Nothing else I could do. You would have done the same.

With an explosion loud enough to break the sound barrier, the explosives went off. They destroyed the entire building and part of nearby buildings as well. Lucky for me, I hid in one of the metal garbage cans outside and was mostly unharmed. I had a couple of cuts and was shaken up. After the initial flames subsided, I got out of the garbage can. I felt very slimy and gross and I think you know why. It is something I do not think I need to explain. I figured I would pack it in for the night, so I went back to my hotel room showered and then slept for most of the night.

I woke up at five in the morning to the sounds of knocking at my door. As I opened the door, a strange tall and buff man pulled a gun out and asked me to follow him. I thought it over and decided that I am not going anywhere but back to bed. He motioned, once again, for me to follow him yelling obscenities at me in Russian. Immediately I reached for the gun, pushed it out of my face, then I spun around breaking his elbow over my shoulder. Then I threw him to the ground after which punches were exchanged. On hitting the ground, I struck the man in the sternum and face more than once. When I got up after striking the man, a short and stubby Russian fellow struck me, with a blunt object, over the back of my shoulders. He broke the object and rendered me unconscious.

I woke up in the middle of the Chihuahuan Desert and I had no visible weapons. I was dressed, which was much to my surprise. I was wearing a black shirt with white stripes and blue jeans. I looked like a basketball referee, yet they left me in my boots. Why they dressed me I will never know. The stupidest thing these kidnappers could have done is left me my boots. They are a similar model to something you would see in a James Bond movie. At the top of the nearest sand dune hill there was one shadowy figure moving about. He was holding some type of weapon pointed in my direction, but that did not bother me.

Within minutes, bullets blared through the sound barrier and passed my head. Quickly, I dove to my left. You would have done the same thing to avoid getting shot. I truly believe you would have. Spontaneously, I propped open the bottom of my left boot and pulled out a one shot derringer style pistol and ran toward the man as I dodged his bullets. He was possibly the worst shooter I have ever come across. That oversized gorilla you always laugh at in the zoo could have taken a better shot than this guy. When I got close enough, I hit the man in the chest. As close as I was to the man I was able to shoot him with moderate accuracy. The bullet put a hole in the man's chest and killed him.

Climbing to the top of the sand dune, I found the man's body engulfed in a lagoon of his own blood. Hit him square in the heart. A lot of you people would have thrown up at the sight of this dead body, but not me. I am used to this kind of horrific scene. It comes with the job. Next to the body was an AK 47 with a removable scope. It is a commonly used communist weapon. I searched the body, but found no identification on him. In his inside coat pocket, I found my .45 automatic handgun with a half loaded clip. One hundred yards in front of me was an army green jeep. To this day I still wonder why they did not kill me before they dropped me in the desert and instead left a man to try to kill me. Must be some kind of game to them. That or they had bigger plans for me. I would have killed me if I was them. I also would have ditched my gun. What do you think? You are probably thinking they were very stupid or that I am one lucky SOB.

I hopped in the jeep, and found the keys were in the passenger seat. How dumb can you be to leave your vehicle keys in the passenger seat? I started the jeep, turned it around, and followed the tracks embedded in the sand. The tracks took me to the nearby highway, which in turn took me back to Santa Fe. Along the way, I noticed a black Porsche Boxer tailing me some couple hundred feet back. I slammed the brakes to slow the car down, so I could get a glimpse of the driver. I almost slammed into the car. I think you would've done the same thing if you were in my shoes. How else was I to find out whom the driver was? Borishkov Medea was the man behind the wheel. Chills went down my spine as I looked through the rear view mirror into his eyes. Staring back at me was the man who killed my father twenty-three years ago.

I never realized it until now, but he was the man in the blue overcoat and green hat. As I drove down the road, I kept thinking that it would be great to capture the one man the CIA has tried on seven occasions to bring in and failed. If the Agency wants me to prove my loyalty than why should I not start now?

Within seconds I sped up to eighty and Borishkov did the same so as not to lose me. I then slammed on my breaks and turned the jeep sideways like the stunt men do in the movies. As human instincts would have it, Medea swerved into the ditch to try to avoid killing himself. Any one of you would have done the same as Medea. I jumped out of the jeep, pulled out my pistol, and charged toward the Porsche. With the injuries that Borishkov had sustained, a few cracked ribs among other small ones, he did the only thing he could. He opened the car door and rolled on top of the pavement, positioning himself on his stomach. I put my gun to his head, took the rope from the trunk of his car, tied his hands behind his back, and drove toward Santa Fe. I stopped off at my hotel and cleaned out my belongings. Immediately after I left my hotel room, I drove Borishkov and myself straight to the hospital followed by the airport the next day.

I told the desk clerk I was escorting a suspect back to Virginia, but she would not believe me. When I showed her my identification, she called her manager. After several calls and without more ado I was booked on the first plane to Richmond. I did not want to have to show her my ID for it caused a big scene when she went to get her supervisor. I did this because I did not want to have to wait five or six hours to maybe a day before the attendant could get me a flight that would take me home. That was the easiest thing to do and you know it.

We arrived in Richmond at twenty-one hundred hours. Being too tired to take Borishkov to headquarters, I got the two of us a hotel room at the airport. I almost took him to my place but I did not want to disturb my wife. Athena would not have been happy if I brought him to our house. He looked like crap and besides my wife and I decided to keep our professional and personal live separate. As if you could not tell that I married a Greek woman. At six in the morning I boarded the next train to Langley, Va.

Upon arriving to the headquarters, I took Medea straight to Aaron Greetox's office. Aaron is my supervisor, or for those of you who do not get that, my boss. He is the guy I have to answer to about everything I do. Aaron was real upset when he saw that I had not gathered useable information or captured Madam Layata. Like everyone else he did not recognize Medea. Medea has several disguises and he looked like something out of a fifties b horror flick.

I took off Medea's coat, glasses, and tore off his fake mustache. After a couple of minutes of staring at Medea, Aaron finally realized whom I had in my custody. Two fellow officers immediately took Borishkov to a holding area. Then I explained everything to Aaron. Minutes later, everyone had heard the news of what I had done. Soon as I left Aaron's office, I was overwhelmed with the number of people who were congratulating me on a job well done. As I said I would, I proved my loyalty and that I was not a sellout or traitor. That is one thing you never get used to and one thing I dislike about working in the CIA. News around here, either god or bad, spreads like a summer wildfire in California forests.

I did not catch Madam Layata in Santa Fe and I do not believe she was ever there to begin with. Either way I will have another chance to do so. Madam Layata and I will meet up again and next time I will be victorious.

Rose Colored City

Let's begin with a little history lesson. Moses was
the man who brought the Israelites out of Egypt and into
the land of Israel. He walked by this city. His brother was
Aaron. For forty years they walked the desert. Where they
walked is what is now Israel and parts of Western Jordan.
In a city known as Petra, Moses supposedly struck a rock
and water flowed from it. It is in the nearby mountains that
some scholars believe Aaron was buried. The city of Petra
is located in what is now Southwestern Jordan and was
built sometime around the sixth century BCE. It was the
capital city of the ancient civilization of the Nabataeans.

The city is carved out of sandstone and into the side
of cliffs, which give each structure a rose red color.
Entrance to the city is only possible through a narrow
ravine called the Siq. The Siq is only accessible from the
eastern side of the city. On entering the city, a place known
as the Treasury becomes visible to the eye. Carved into the
side of the mountain, it is a Greek like structure that is
similar looking to the Parthenon. It is given the name of
Treasury due to the myths that surround its use. Some say
the Pharaoh, during the time of the Pentateuch, used this
place to hide parts of his massive wealth. Others believe in

thieves who stored their loot there. Either story may be true but we know that at some point it was used as a tomb.

Another famous site at Petra is just to the northwest of the Treasury and is called the Monastery. It was built by the Nabataeans several centuries after most of the city was built and it was used as a place for religious ceremonies. The Rose Red City has several intricate waterways to bring water into the city from rivers miles away. The city also contains many different tombs and the Romans built a road from the city back to Rome itself. When Rome converted to Christianity, the Rose Colored City became a papal state with its own bishop presiding over its Christian followers. In a letter from Cyril, the bishop of Jerusalem, it is known that a major earthquake struck the city in 363 CE/AD. The city was lost for centuries until it was discovered in 1812 by a Swiss explorer. Lawrence of Arabia defended the city against the Turkish by using the Siq during WWI.

Now what is the reason for me giving you a history lesson about a place east of the Dead Sea? I will get to the answer for that question in just a little bit. First I need to give you another lesson on a group of people you may or may not have contact with in your life. This lesson is what I like to call RFDWT. The acronym stands for Rules for Dealing with Terrorists. Take plenty of notes for you may someday need them when if you are ever in the field. They are not that hard to remember and may even save a life or two. One thing you must ALWAYS remember when interacting with terrorists is the following: an action with thought saves a life, while an action without thought takes the life of many. Do not ever forget that phrase for it may save you if ever you are in the field. If you do not understand it then take a moment to think about it and the meaning will come to you. These rules you are about to learn are not in some textbook and you will not find them in the "FBI playbook." These are my rules and if you have been in this business as long as I have, just as I have, you will find what works and what does not.

Follow my rules and you will do just fine. That is even if you are told not to do something because that is not how you are supposed to do things. It's like the FBI rules for hostage negotiations. They have a set of rules agents are supposed to follow, and agents are expected to follow them in order regardless of how the situation is playing out. These rules of mine may not be what the CIA wants you to follow, and these rules may not be the way some people around here do things. Adaptation is key component when one interacts with terrorists because sometimes the steps in the "Playbook" get disrupted and you have to improvise.

Some of the big wigs around her cannot see that or they are so into themselves they do not want to hear they just might be wrong. Sometimes they are just trying to cover their own butt. By the way, I use the term playbook loosely for even that is subject to one's own interpretation. Stick around the spy game long enough and you will see what I am talking about.

Now let's get down to business. Rule number one is not solely based on the USA's mandate for handling terrorists though that is part of the reason for the rule. Rule one state's that you DO NOT negotiate with terrorists. You will never get them to sit down for that meeting and you will not win. You do not negotiate because of rule number two which states that terrorist's DO NOT negotiate. Why is this? That is a valid question for you to ask. The answer lies in rule number three. Rule three states that they make demands and expect everyone to pay with no exceptions. Their demands can be anything from wanting troops pulled out of a country to stopping talks with a group of people. The US and CIA policy is not to give in to their demands at all costs. So what happens if you do not accept their demands? Rules four and five will answer that question.

Rule four is that terrorist's always have bargaining chips. They will use these chips to get you to do what you want. Most of their chips are hostages or explosives placed in some location as to do maximum damage and cause maximum death with plenty of panic. They may even send body parts as a reminder of what they can do if their demands are not met. Sometimes a small bomb will go off as a reminder that a grander chain of events will ensue if you do not give them what they want. Rule five: attempt to remove their bargaining chip or bad things will happen. Hostages will possibly die or innocent lives will be lost. Mostly this is for a political cause or some religious reasons and I know that may seem whacked to you but it is true. If it means reaching their goals a terrorist organization will stop at nothing to get what they want and if they cannot get their agenda fulfilled they will follow rule number six.

Always remember rule number six which is that terrorist's DON NOT LEAVE WITNESSES! Why do they leave no witnesses? It is because of rule seven stating that terrorists' willingly will kill anyone including themselves. If they have a hostage they will have no regrets in killing them and cutting their losses. Sometimes they will have no problem in killing themselves rather than be captured and rot in a cell in some dark hole. Death means nothing to them. One must remember rule eight because terrorists do not follow the rules for they make their own. The CIA teaches operatives a set of guidelines for how they want you to handle terror groups. Terrorists do not care about the CIA and they do not use the same steps or patterns when they make their moves. They are not like a book you can read or a movie you can quote. They do not do the same things twice and they could care less about laws or signed agreements like the Geneva Convention. They do what they want because they follow the rules of their leader and no one else.

Rule nine is taken right out of the old police adage to catch a criminal one must think like a criminal. In our case we are going to substitute the word terrorist for the word criminal. A key to winning a confrontation with someone like this is to do the exact opposite of what everyone expects you to do. You need to change things up periodically. You do not want to be an open book everyone's read. If someone always knows what you are going to do they will be able to adjust and counter everything you do and you will always end up losing.

When pursuing terrorists, anything that may happen most likely will. That is rule ten. If you think it can happen or you can picture it in your mind then you had better be ready for it. They are the most unpredictable group of people you will encounter on the job. Most time when you face them in the field you are entering their playground and they have had more time to prepare for you then you have to survey the land and plan your attack. Therefore, you must expect traps or planted explosive waiting to take you and your team out. If you do not expect them and other extreme things then someone will be attending your funeral.

Number eleven: Until you have captured or killed every terrorist on your mission, they will always have control of the situation. Take them out or be taken out for there is no other option. Remember to keep any hostages you are after as safe as you can. Yet, use any force necessary to take out your targets. That applies for all hostage situations and not just ones involving terrorists. They are always on defense and that means they have the upper hand which means you do not have control of the situation.

Rule twelve is an important one to remember in everything you do if you are in the field. It states: always know who and what is around you. Pay attention to all the details that you can. Watch what people do, who they are talking to, and what things go by your position. If someone looks threatening or out of place then you should pay close attention to them. When you enter a building to clear it you should follow the triangle exit plan. The triangle plan means that when you enter a building or any place of social gathering you should look for three places in which you can exit if need be. One exit should be the way you came in and the other two should make a triangle. When hunting terrorists this plan will help you if retreating are needed. Whenever I enter anywhere I use the triangle plan.

The thirteenth and final rule sums up just about all the previous rules that I have talked about. The last rule to remember is terrorists can make any situation, either from good or bad, go to hell faster than anybody can run. You need to be ready for anything to happen. Think before you react but do not take a long time to react. I always follow the mantras that if you play to win you look to lose and if you come to dominate you play for the win. That is how I take on each mission that is given to me. It is a philosophy that you can learn from and take to the field.

Let's tie these two lessons together for those of you who are curious about what I am trying to lead up to. In June of 1983 a husband and wife team of archaeologists from Arizona State University were on the end of a sabbatical working at the site of Petra (the Rose Colored City). They were looking for evidence of the burial of

Aaron, the brother of Moses. They thought they could find evidence that he was buried in the nearby mountains. At the same time I was in Israel finishing up a joint mission with Mossad. I got the call on my way out of the hotel I was staying in. My boss, Aaron, told me that the US government had just been given a video demanding that the US stop all sanctions on Jordan and stop chasing members of the Chosen Ones or the two American professors would be executed.

Now the Chosen Ones are an Islamic extremist terrorist group based out of southern Jordan. The US had created sanctions against Jordan for some of its officials had been harboring known members of the Chosen Ones terrorist group. The Jordanian government as a whole would like to eradicate the Chosen Ones. They have bombed several embassies throughout the Middle East including those of the US and Britain. They also wanted the release of Akbar Mila-Ha Jaobakea who is the group number two. Akbar, currently, is in a US prison camp after a failed embassy bombing last year.

The leader of the Chosen Ones is Ominia Romitti a Kulo Kula. He sometimes goes by Orakk for short. The video showed the two professors tied to chairs bloody and beaten with the woman sexually assaulted. The room was dimly lit and the walls were made of sun-dried mud bricks. None of the terrorist faces were seen on the video but their voices were heard giving the demands. My mission as I was told: Bring the hostages home safe at all costs and if you get caught your government denies ever knowing you. You will learn if you have not already that the last part of my mission is CIA standard on every overseas operation.

Before I entered Jordan I met with an agent near the Israel/Jordon boarder and was given a US military M1911A1 pistol with one clip in the chamber and three spare clips. If you know anything about the pistol you would be thinking, like me, that the amount of ammo I was given was not a lot. The gun uses .45 ACP caliber rounds and carries a seven round clip with an amount of twenty-eight bullets given to me. Even you can see this is not a lot of ammo for such a huge undertaking. I was also given a modified Seiko Chronograph watch which would show up to three heat signatures at a distance of a quarter mile. It also has a detonation mode allowing a huge flash of light for a few seconds, blinding all who look at it for a couple of moments. It will destroy the watch in the process. The last thing I was given was a small amount of plastic explosive that I could conceal under my belt buckle. You got to love the tech boys of the Agency.

The last thing the agent told me was that I had to sneak into Jordan and if I wanted any more weapons or gadgets, I would have to steal them or take them from the dead. Soon enough you will learn that that is standard procedure on sensitive operations like this one. Have you all been paying attention? If you have not been then let me remind you that what just happened was exactly rules one through four and that I am about to embark on executing rule number five. For those of you that are paying close attention to the rules, good job.

I entered Jordan using my Russian alias whose name is Romani Gudenchki. Only two other people alive know that Romani and I am the same person. Not even the CIA knows we are one in the same. This alias is so well done that even the Russian government believes he is a real person and not an American spy's cover name. How did I get the alias you ask? Well, that is another story for another time.

My first stop took me form the outskirts of Jerusalem to the Jordanian city of Al Karak. The trip took me about a day and a half and I rested in a shoddy rat infested hotel for the night. The next morning I took a quarter of a day ride through the desert to the site of the Rose Colored City (Petra). The temperature of the day was seventy nine degrees Fahrenheit. I entered the city taking a ride through a narrow passage way called the Siq. Next I came upon a structure called the Treasury. The Treasury has a beautiful reddish tone due to the sandstone color of the mountainside it was carved from. I then took a trip to what is called The High Place of Sacrifice which can be found south of the Roman Theater. This was the place that Dr. Eric and Jocelyn Flauntain were taken from by the Chosen Ones. There was not much to see and not many clues of where the Flauntain's were taken. I took the rest of the day to tour Petra like a tourist.

Once the tour was over I headed back to the modern city that was built as a tourist town due to the many people wanting to see the beauty of the Rose Colored City. You think I am taking this moment as a vacation but I assure you I am not. One has to enjoy the places they are visiting or the job causes one to go crazy or breakdown. I woke up the next morning and went to a nearby café to get breakfast. The marketplace was full of people bargaining for fruits and vegetable, clothing, or other necessities. It was only eight in the morning but the market was packed fuller than Madison Square Gardens during a Knicks Celtics game.

I ordered a tea and contemplated the plan I was going to put into action. I drink tea because I cannot stand coffee. The one thing I had to plan out was how I was going to explain a Russian tourist asking questions about two American archaeologists. If you remember I entered Jordan as a Russian named Romani Gudenchki and not Joey Scapeotto. Now I would like you to take a moment and think of a plan that you would put into action. Bet it is nothing like what I am about to do.

I spent minutes contemplating what I was going to do and then I left the café. I made my way through the crowds of people and headed down the alley across form the café. At the end of the alley was a shady shop. The wooden door was scratched and beaten up. As I entered the shop I could see a small bearded Arabic man with a large white turban behind the counter. I noticed that this was an Islamic prayer rug shop. The walls were lined with rugs with mosaic patterns and deep toned colors. They were made from a cheap material and the looked as if they would become tattered after just a few uses. They were not nearly worth the price and I do not see how people would pay for one of them. You could find a better quality rug for half the price back in the market. The good quality silk rugs were behind the counter and cost twice of the rugs along the walls.

Standing at the counter was a tall giant of a man

talking to the owner of the shop at the counter. I could see that the giant was holding a shopping list. It was not the kind of shopping list you think of or maybe it is. I am six feet tall and the giant had to be a foot taller than I. You would have thought he was creepy too. The giant walked right passed me and for a moment I thought about leaving.

Soon as the giant left the shop the owner pulled a magnum pistol from under the counter and pointed it in my direction. He could tell I was not a native Jordanian because my hair was not dark and sun bleached enough as well as my skin color was too white. I am glad that I look more like my English and Dutch mother than my Italian father or I could not pass as a Russian. He kept the gun pointed at me and started yelling something at me in Arabic. I speak five languages (English, German, Russian, Spanish, and broken Mandarin), and unfortunately Arabic is mot one of them. The CIA will mostly send you to places where you know the language and customs of the people even though on occasion you will be sent to a place out of your comfort zone.

I started yelling back at him in Russian but I do not think he understood any of the words I spoke. I do not think it mattered what I said for he kept waving the gun at me. The air got heavy and the tension became thick as our situation heated up. For a moment I believed he was going to put a bullet in my skull and go about his day. After the owner could not take anymore he spoke loud and clear asking me what in the hell I was doing in his shop. His English had a heavy Middle Eastern accent and he asked if I understood him.

At this point I had to become the best actor and salesperson you have ever seen in action. While on the job you will become your aliases like an actor learning a role; you have to know your alias as good if not better than you know yourself. You better know your alias and you need to sell it as if you were selling heaven to the devil himself. The hardest problem with this job is not letting your alias become a part of you for you can easily lose the core of whom you really are. It will consume you and at some point you will self-destruct because of it.

I told the owner I was a former Russian soldier looking to sell large quantities of weapons and information on the black market. I knew he had the information on the black market for the list the giant was holding contained several weapons on it. The black market was going to be my ticket to succeed on this mission. Intelligence that was given to the CIA by way of MI6 tells that the Chosen Ones own the black market in this part of the world and I knew that would be my way to find the archaeologists. I told him the information that I had was on US trade routes and spy operations between the countries of Iraq and Syria. You had better not DARE think of ME as a traitor or someone who would sell out US agents.

My intelligence was really a mixture of Russian smuggling routes and local guerilla trade posts. If you are a good salesperson you can sell anything to anyone anytime. The same holds true for agents in the field. You must be able to get anyone to believe any story you tell them the moment you start talking. I got the owner to believe my intelligence was about American spy routes and drop off points and not what it really was. If you cannot or will not become a good liar then you only have but two choices. You can become an analyst for the Agency or you can get out and try a new line of work.

The owner seemed a little reserved in wanting to tell me where to go next. I guess it had to do with him not really knowing me all that well and having no trust in me. Would you blame him? I would not. If I had to guess, I would think this shop was a front for the Chosen Ones. He told me that if I really needed to unload my weapons quickly that I was to travel southeast to the territory capital of Ma'an. I was to take road thirty-five south until I hit road fifteen then follow it until I entered Ma'an. Do you know how long that was going to take me? It was about as long if not longer than a car ride from Miami to Chicago.

The owner of the rug shop only gave me the name of a person whom I should speak with. He also told me that if I wanted to find this man I should look for him to be having lunch at one of three places in Ma'an around one o'clock. The man I was looking for was none other than arms dealer and Chosen Ones member Baksaune al Zelkare. Baksaune is an Iranian born member of the Chosen Ones who fancies himself as a world class scientist. He looks like an average Middle-Eastern with a head twice as big. He studied chemistry at Université Claude Bernard Lyon 1 located in Lyon, France and graduated in 1975. He is a stocky man missing his front tooth because of a fight over family pride.

He met Ominia, leader of the Chosen Ones, when he was working for the Iranian government on ways to improve oil drilling in the country. Ominia was contracted by the Iranian government to help with construction of a new type of oil drill and he met Baksaune while on the job. Ominia Romitti a Kulo Kula was born in Ma'an, Jordan and graduated in 1968 from Technion – Israel Institute of Technology located in Haifa, Israel. Ominia began preaching in Iran around 1973 and formed the Chosen Ones by 1976, where he moved the group to Southern Jordan and began his acts of terrorism against anyone with a Western viewpoint. Ominia is a tall man who is as thin as Twiggy. He wears his beard past his elbows and his face shows his age to be ten years older than he is. He sticks out in a crowd for he has a nose bigger than Jimmy Durante.

The reason I was given three places where I might be able to find Baksaune is because he is a paranoid borderline schizophrenic. What makes him one of Ominia's top advisors are he will not make deals with anyone without a background check that would make the FBI envious. Even you can see that my plan was going to have to be bulletproof or I might end up dead. The worst part of it is I am trying to find a man who deals in weapons to sell him guns I do not have. I will figure something out when I get beyond the first meeting with Baksaune.

I woke up the day after I arrived in Ma'an and decided to stake out one place I was given. I made my mind up that I was going to come to the same place every day until Baksaune showed up. It took me two days to meet him and I used the time to come up with my pitch. This is one of those moments that you either got it or you do not and you can practice till you are blue but even that may not be enough. You have to learn to do this on your own because even I cannot teach it to you.

What would you say to Baksaune? Me, well I introduced myself and gave him the same story as I told to the rug shop owner about being a Russian with weapons and information to sell. The restaurant had around eight tables filled with people dinning for lunch with ten plus seats around a bar at the far south end of the place. The place was noisy with normal lunch time restaurant chatter. Baksaune looked uninterested and gave me some bull about not wanting to do business with new clients, at this time. As he ate his fish I could see the veins popping out of his enlarged neck as he told me emphatically that he did not want to do business.

The events that happened next were totally unexpected but at the same time they made me a friend for the moment in Baksaune. I left his lunch table and headed for the door thinking that may plans would have to change. It was at that moment that a slightly unshaven average height Jordanian with dark hair came walking into the restaurant and headed straight for Baksaune's table. He was wearing a brownish suede shirt with dark jeans as he reached into his sport coat pocket. Immediately, one of Baksaune's body guards stood up as the mystery man called

36

for Baksaune to get up and come outside with him.

The muscular guard was shoved out of the way and back into his seat. The guard got up and took a swing at the mystery man who grabbed his arm and did a Chuck Norris style flip to the guard throwing him on the floor. He then took out a small caliber revolver and killed the guard as well as the other guard sitting next to Baksaune. I could not make out what the mystery man and Baksaune talked about because they spoke in Arabic but I understood when the man said he was from the Jordanian Special Police Force. The Special Police Force in Jordan is primarily responsible for antiterrorism and the government would love to kill all members of the Chosen Ones as well as drive them out of commission and the country.

I did the first thing that came to my mind and as the scene unfolded in front of me I took a moment to think it over. I know what you are thinking, for I can see it in your eyes and yes it was the right thing to do for my mission. As the two walked passed me I stepped in front of the police force officer as if I was a drunken sailor and pushed him back a few steps. I stumbled to my feet and slurred some words like I had just drunk five Mia Tai's. Funny thing is I have not had a single drink but if I did it would be a Mia Tai as my drink of choice. The officer helped me to my feet and told me to get out of this place and go sleep off the drunkenness.

I fell into him again and he got very mad. As he pushed me off him my right fist slammed into his abdomen followed by a fast twist of the gun. My motion was fast enough and such that the slide of the gun came off the barrel so that the gun would not fire. Next, I proceeded to whale on him like Ali hitting Frazier during the end of the Thrilla in Manila. Now I am not like some of you who are Kung Fu masters like Chuck Norris. Though, I can fight well if I have to because of the almost twenty years of boxing training that I have. Soon as the officer dropped to his knees Baksaune and I ran out the door and got into his car. We sped out of the crowded neighborhood and headed southwest out of town.

I could see that Baksaune was a little shaken by what had happened and he kept thanking me the entire car ride. Baksaune decided to reconsider my offer and he dropped my off at my hotel room. He told me he would pick me up in a day or two after he talked things over with his boss. This was my break in the mission and I was hoping to be taken to see Ominia even if I was blindfolded. I thought that if I met Ominia, the Flauntain's would not be far off. Would you have fought the officer knowing that afterwards you would be wanted by the police?

Two days later, I was picked up by Baksaune and just as I thought they put a black breathable bag over my head as we drove to the meeting place. I was told that Ominia was more interested in the information on spy routes than he was in the weapons I made them believe I had. What a relief knowing I was not going to have to produce a pile of weapons from the nothing I really had. During the last day that I waited to be picked up I called my boss (my handler) Aaron Greetox to fill him in on what was going on. I could imagine his boney cheeks and brown eyes flaring up as he heard what I had done. Man, was the CIA brass angry to find out that the Jordanian police wanted a man with my description in custody. Aaron also gave me the name of a US double agent working for the Russians that were in the area.

We headed to a compound located a few miles north of town. In the distance I could faintly smell rotten eggs. The smell was really hydrogen sulfide. It is the same smell you may have when you turn on your sink. In small quantities it can be harmless. If injected or ingested in larger quantities it can become a toxin in the body and may cause the nervous system to become paralyzed and even shut down. In my head I hoped this was not going to be the way in which they were planning to execute the Flauntain's. Even you can see that would be a horrible way to die.

I met with Ominia in some dirty and trashy half lit room filled with papers all over the floor and plates of partially eaten hummus on the table in the middle of the room. Ominia offered me a plate but I had just eaten a large sandwich. To my surprise and probably to some of you as well, Ominia wanted to take a look at the weapons that I supposedly had but he valued the information more. I was lied to by a group of terrorists. Like that should be a surprise. Yeah right. We talked for a while about our beliefs and about what I was doing in Jordan. I told him it was to sell weapons and information so I could make a run from some mobsters I owed money. I mentioned that I though Jordan would be a place out of the mobs radar so they may not try to kill me before I got all I owed them. Ominia bought the part about me owing money to the mob but not why I was in Jordan.

Ominia kept asking questions about why I was in Jordan and not some European city. I kept insisting that my choice of country had to do with my privacy and safety. After a while he inquired about the information that was for sale. I told him about a small guerilla group in northwest

Saudi Arabia that was encroaching on the Chosen Ones
territory in Jordan. They were recruiting soldiers for their
cause and many of the people they were forcing to join
them were from refugee camps near the Jordan Saudi
Arabian border. One thing people forget, including you, is
that just because terrorist groups have a similar view does
not mean they are best of friends and will share territories
or potential recruits. The strangest view of the Chosen Ones
is that they do not believe in involving refuges and will go
out of their way to avoid refugee camps. Do not let that
sway your opinion of them for they are still crazy
murderous extremists. They are still terrorists in the eyes of
everyone who is not one of them. I also dropped the name
of the double agent I was given.

   Ominia insisted that he would not pay me until he
had thoroughly looked into the information that I gave him.
Guards proceeded to escort me out of the compound
building toward a big jeep the size of a Jeep Cherokee. On
my way out of the building I was in I got a good look at a
room that was being prepared for a video. They were also
escorting two bodies toward the room. Each body was
wearing a bag on their head with their hands tied and the
female was screaming about wanting to be let go while the
male was quiet. Ominia and company must be getting

impatient with the US' unwillingness to comply with their demands and I feared I was running out of time.

I tried to ask about them but all I got was a cold shoulder and a reply that it was not for me to concern myself with such matters. We left the room and entered a dark hallway with three industrial size fans attached to the walls and they were blowing slowly with a constant whooshing sound. As I was being put into the jeep I caught a glimpse of a slightly tall woman with bright colored hair. She was a beautiful looking woman and for a moment I caught her looking back at me. She looked to be in her late twenties to middle thirties and some of the guards were drooling over her Vogue cover beautiful looks. If this woman was who my brain kept telling me that she was then I was looking at some serious trouble with a possibly blown cover.

Only two people know that I am Romani Gudenchki. One is a member of MI6, Daniel Macradin, whose alias is Nikolai Gudenchki the brother of Romani. The reality is that Daniel and I are not brothers and he is six years older than I. The other is a Russian spy who goes by the code name Madam. The CIA calls her Madam not because she is a young lady but because she looks younger than she is, she can be very seductive when she wants, and can make one believe she has the charm akin to that of a sixteen to twenty-one year old southern belle.

The reason I am mentioning this about my alias is that if my eyes are not playing desert style tricks on me, than my brain and my feet are right to tell the rest of my body that I should get the hell out of Ma'an before the next time my wife sees me it will be at my funeral. If the woman I just saw is who I think she is then the right thing to do is hit the road for she could have all the Chosen Ones' hunting me down like the mob chasing Frankenstein.

Before I could do anything they shoved me into the vehicle and we took off for town. I had to rethink my plan if I was going to get the Flauntain's out alive. I got dropped off at my hotel and they told me that they wanted to see a sample of my weapons by sundown tomorrow. I can see some of you think I am screwed but that is just because you do not know me well enough to say anything else. I told the desk clerk to wake me just after sunrise and went to my room to clean up for dinner. I went back to the restaurant where I met Baksaune and ordered a falafel on pita bread with a baklawa for dessert with a Mai Tai on the rocks. It's at this point that my outlook on the day changed for the better.

A cop was drinking way too much, and he was

becoming loudly boisterous about a pretty young woman eating in the back of the place with her new flame. I bumped into him as he stumbled around the bar yelling obscenities to the woman in the back. I do not think I have to tell you the things he called her. He seemed heartbroken over the woman for leaving him for the guy she was eating with. As I bumped into him, I took the badge out of his pocket and kept on walking toward the restroom. I then left the restaurant and headed to the nearest precinct. I bet you have no idea what I am about to do, so take some notes.

Using CIA info I knew that the local police had just raided a compound full of weapons and ammo belonging to the Chosen Ones. I was going to inquire about those weapons and then I was going to borrow them for my next piece of my plan. I entered the precinct and told the desk clerk why I was there. I gave the clerk a story about wanting to take the weapons to be destroyed and that I was running behind schedule which would explain why I was there so late at night. After showing him my badge, he told me to come back in the morning and he would get the guns ready.

I came back to the precinct at eight in the morning and went through the same spiel with an older woman who made several calls and told me to go to storage lockup. The man running the storage did not know of what was being told to him, but after a long persuading conversation, he reluctantly released a truckload of weapons into my possession. I took the weapons to the place where I was told I could meet with Baksaune. Baksaune got into his car and I followed them to the compound just north of Ma'an.

This was it. It was the moment before I had to make up my mind on what I was going to do to find the Flauntain's. After this deal I was going to be paid for my wares and be sent on my way with no reason to ever be in the compound again. All of you who get to be in the field will have at least one of these moments and it is what you do in them that you will see your mission either live or die.

The moment I entered the compound Ominia was waiting for me with a warm greeting. His face looked beyond sun dried and his brown eyes looked very tired and frustrated from the ordeal with the US. I feared time was not on my side and that if I was to leave without the Flauntain's their families will never see them again. I think in this situation you would feel the same way as me.

Ominia test fired several random assault weapons but expressed interest in wanting rocket propelled firearms above all else. Just my luck that I had not one on hand but I gave him a completely false account that if given a week or two I could get a full shipment for him. He did not buy it and told me not to scramble over it. He saw right through my story and then again I did not sell it as best I could. We all have those moments and even you know it.

If you can think back a few moments to when I described my Rules For Dealing With Terrorists, providing you paid attention to me back then, you would know that I was going to be thrust into rule ten and that I would have to use rule nine taking rule eleven into account. If you wrote them down then I am delighted you are good students. If you forgot to copy down the rules, then may God have mercy on you if my situation becomes yours.

Ominia called for his men to go inside and leave the two of us to discuss the terms of this deal. Six or seven men went into the main compound building and I was left alone with Ominia. Immediately, he had me empty my pockets and throw the contents at his feet. I complied and at his feet I laid my pistol, a small pocket sized camera, my vehicle keys, and a pack of cinnamon flavored tic tacs. He grabbed my pistol and pointed it at my face screaming about my deception and called me a spy who will die for the world to see how the US cannot be trusted.

I can see you are wondering 'how could this

happen?' How could he know you are an agent of the CIA? Remember that good looking woman I told you I saw when last I left the compound. She knows I am not a Russian and that my story is full of not one single truth. The first time I met her I was on a five person team extracting a Cambodian political and his family who were defecting to the US back in 1975. This woman, Anna Layata, killed my four teammates and left me for dead. If not for a doctor running from Pol Pot's army I would be six feet under and never would have met my wife, because her brother led that team.

Ever since Anna found out that I had not taken an eternal sleep that day, the Russian weasel has been trying to send me to an early grave. I should have put a bullet into her skull when I saw her in the compound, but sometimes the things we do are not as we wish. She is the reason I was in this predicament, but she will not be the death of me! NOT TODAY! I can see you think you know what I was about to do. Let's see if you are right by telling you what I actually did.

I started to laugh at the notion of anything Ominia just said. I started to tell him about how she was the spy playing him and that everything she said about me was a euphemistical invention of her twisted imagination. Ominia waved that gun in my face claiming I was the wolf in sheep's clothing and he gave me a few moments to explain my real reason for being there.

I told him my real story and he laughed at me calling it another lie. I told him to put that gun away and to finish the deal, but as the incompetent fool that he is the weapon stayed in my face. He pushed the barrel into my forehead and used it to push me back a step all the while screaming at me to get on my knees and turn around. Even like you, I am not sure if Ominia wanted to kill me or use me as bait to get Akbar Mila-Ha Jaobakea released from the hole he was hidden. Either way I was not going to find out the answer.

I turned my body as to get on my knees. Instead of hitting my knees my right hand chopped into his wrist, while my left hand shoved the gun in the opposite direction of my other hand. The gun flew out of his hand and on to the ground. I then twisted his arm into a bar extending his elbow, while twice hitting under his arm right under his collar bone. Everyone heard the loud scream as I heard his arm pop and dislocate at his shoulder blade. Before anyone could get outside to stop me I dove to the ground, grabbed my gun as I spun around getting up to my knees, and a shot resonated as I put a .45 caliber hole into Ominia's head.

I grabbed my camera, which is slim and grey while looking like a pistol clip, and slid the two sides together to take a picture of Ominia Romitti a Kulo Kula as his blood waters the ground to which he fell. I then ran to the right of the main compound building heading toward the three smaller structures. I dove behind a couple of wooden crates that offer very little protection. I took the round rim of the face of my watch and turned it a click to the right. The watch face became black and on its bottom I could see three small green radar colored dots indicating that there were a few men behind me running in my direction.

They were yelling at on another in Arabic making a strategy to take me out. In just a moment I was about to feel rule number thirteen in action. The building next to me was a sand colored brick like two story structure that looked like it was used as a living quarters for some of the higher ranking members. I dove through the window and noticed to my left a hundred feet was the front entrance to this house. Straight ahead I saw a kitchen and a window overlooking the washtub propped against the wall.

From the front entrance a sharp left takes one up the stairs to the second floor. The door, the washtub window, and the window I just came in are my triangle of exits out of this building. You do remember the triangle exit plan?

My watch radar was showing at least two bodies near or up the stairs and one in the kitchen ahead of me.

I chose the path up the stairs and found myself firing three shots as two terrorists dropped dead down the stairs. Immediately, I found that I was being pushed back down the stairs do to a barrage of AK-47 bullets heading in my direction. Someone shouted in Arabic. It was most likely for me to surrender. Soon as the bullets stopped blazing my way I heard the clicking of the gun indicating the shooter was reloading. At this point I did what even you would do by creeping up the stairs and putting two shots into the man down the end of the hall. Loading the last bullet into the chamber I replaced the empty clip.

Going down the narrow hallway I could see four rooms that needed clearing. The first room to my right was empty. I kicked in the door to my left and I could feel someone behind it. As I entered I slammed the bottom of my pistol into the terrorists face putting him out cold. I proceeded to do the same for the next two rooms at the end of the hall. I came up empty in the last two rooms. After entering the last room, I could hear and my watch told me that at least three men were racing up the stairs toward me like a lion chasing a zebra.

Even you could see I was left with only two options. Jump two stories out the window in the room behind me or head back toward the stairs going through a group of armed angry men who want nothing more than to hang me from the ceiling by my toes while they beat me with knotted ropes till I bleed to death. What do you think you would do? I fired a shot down the hallway and the group scurried down the stairs.

I ran out and grabbed the bloody body holding it against me as I hid between it and the wall. The terrorists started firing at me, but all they hit was their dead friend. One shot and I had another one more dead. I made my way back into the room, while dragging the dead body with me. You may think of me as very stupid or daring for what I did next.

I heaved the dead body out the window followed by the box spring in the corner of the room. Then, like a stuntman jumping onto a giant air bag, I dove out the window landing on the mattress and rolling to the ground. For a moment my body was racked with pain. Yes it hurt for a long time, but I fought through it like you might have to someday.

From under my belt I took the plastic explosive and took a very deep breath. Yeah, I know I am lucky it has not gone off yet. If I were you I would have thought the same thing. I placed the small explosive close to the building and I pushed all the buttons on my watch as I rotated the clock face one click to the right and placed it on the plastic explosive. I had about five seconds before the watch would set off a blinding flash as it detonates giving off a small electric like charge. The charge was going to be enough to detonate the explosive

Soon as I dropped the watch I ran, no joke, right around a 4.65 forty yard dash. The explosion sent massive pieces of the building flying into the air as if they were shrapnel. The explosion was bigger than it should have been. The small piece of explosive that I placed should not have tore the whole building except for the part that on the other side of the wall was the gas stove in the kitchen. Bodies were throughout the compound flying high in the sky.

The blast left a small sized hole in the outer wall of the main compound edifice. I ran and dove into the hole, landing on a hard sandy surface. I looked like I had been shot several times and thrown out of a moving airplane falling into a landfill. Before the blast the room would have been nearly dark with one small high iron bared window for sunlight. The entrance was covered with a large metal door similar to one seen in solitary confinement at a maximum security prison. Against the wall, near the door, was two mangled steam producing boilers probably used for heating several nearby rooms.

I hid in the corner by one of the boilers and proceeded to fire two shots at the metal door. Then I waited patiently for what felt like minutes. If you were in my shoes you would have done the same thing, and if you think like me you would be right. The noise of my bullets caused one dumb curious idiot to open the metal door and receive a complimentary bullet in his head courtesy of yours truly.

I picked up the dead man's AK-47 and searched his body finding one spare clip and a flash grenade. With my ammo situation it was the smart thing to do, and even you know it! To my right was the three fans I noticed the other day, and at the end of the hall was the room where I met with Ominia. I think that room was his personal quarters. Around the corner at the end of the hall was another pathway leading to the room where I saw the Flauntain's being taken the last time I was here.

In that room there was a table surrounded by two empty evenly spaced chairs and a camera pointed in that direction. Behind the chairs was a hanging tapestry with the Chosen Ones insignia. Their insignia is on a green tapestry with the word Allah in Arabic script in the background with a globe and the Arabic word Salaam in the foreground. Underneath the globe is the phrase Allah's chosen ones written in Arabic script.

Their insignia is based on the Chosen Ones philosophy that Allah told Ominia that he was the chosen one to bring peace to the world in the way that Mohammad had envisioned, and all that oppose this vision need to be eradicated from the planet. The Chosen Ones terror organization came about out of the teachings of Ominia and his ability to get others to believe he was chosen by Allah and follow him. Even I agree with you that the entire notion of any of this being at all true about Orakk being "chosen" is a load of malarkey. The only truth about it is that there are people gullible enough to believe it.

I turned around to a rifle in my face with a man ordering my weapon dropped and my hand in the air. I dropped my rifle and while bringing my hand up I pulled the pin from the flash grenade. The two men in the room backed up a couple of steps with a scared look in their eyes. If you were them I think you would have the same fear that they most likely had. They backed up as if I had pulled the pin on a live grenade and not a flash one. I threw the grenade into the air, slid under the table, covered my ears while closing my eyes, and waited a few moments until the grenade went off.

I lay on my stomach as I grabbed my pistol out of the back of my belt and fired two shots in the chest at the first disoriented terrorist. To the ground dead he fell. In order to survive you would have done the same thing and you cannot convince me otherwise. I fired the last shot of the clip into the upper thigh of the second terrorist in the room.

He dropped to his knees and tried to fire at me while screaming in pain. I threw the table over onto its side for a little protection though it was not as much as it looks in the movies. I loaded my pistol with my third of four clips and readied for my next move. As soon as the terrorist started reloading his rifle, I jumped into action. I hopped over the table, ran across the room, and slide feet first baseball style across the floor grabbing my dropped rifle.

Turning toward the bleeding and screaming man, I unloaded everything in the rifles clip thus placing the man on permanent dream street. That is, if you know what I mean? Loading the rifle with the one spare clip I had, I made sure to remove the two clips from the men I just shot. Lucky for me both of the clips were just inserted into the rifles I took them from, so they were fully loaded clips. I peeked out and around the entrance to the room I was in. Seeing no one, I entered the hallway. I crouched aiming the gun, while I listened to the sound around me.

If you cannot tone your ears to differentiate between the different sounds you hear in the field, then you had better find a desk job for your body will eventually fail you on a mission. One who does not listen to the sounds around them are no different from one who shows up to a movie in the theaters an hour late. Both are present but have no idea what is going on and therefore they are lost. In this business if one is lost one is as good as dead. You can quote me on that.

Hearing nothing but near silence around me, I turned the corner and headed down the dimly lit hallway. The sounds of the fans slowly running was a little nerving as I neared the room with the big metal door. Just as I neared the main entrance to the building I was in, a terrorist with a pump shotgun bumped into me. We both stumbled back a step, and if it was not for him needing to pump his gun to load a shell I would have acquired a soccer ball sized hole in my chest. .

I pumped him full of more lead than a number two pencil. You can count another terrorist down. I dropped the rifle I possessed because in this situation I prefer a shotgun any day. The shotgun had sixteen extra shells plus a full eight in its chamber. On the side of the shotgun was a mounted flashlight and a removable rifle scope. Now can you answer me, who in their right mind thinks a shotgun needs a scope? In close quarters a shotgun is a point and fire weapon that if you get hit by it you will most likely be dead as a result.

From the entrance to the building, with my back to it, I took a left and turned the corner to crossfire from a couple of terrorist waiting for me. One of them kept firing down the hallway as the other ran after me. Soon as the terrorist turned the corner after me, body met shotgun shell at less than two-hundred yards. Bet you can guess which one won.

The other terrorist, down the hall, seeing his friend splatter all over the place threw a pineapple grenade into the corner trying to blow me to the moon. I think you would have done the same thing as me. I grabbed the grenade, like a stupid fool, and threw it out the entrance as it exploded in the air moments after I let go of it.

Readying myself to grab my pistol, I fired a random shotgun cover shot and the terrorist ducked out of the way. For the moment he stopped firing to avoid getting hit. I turned the corner waiting for him to get up. As he did, three pistol bullets shot his way with one missing and two hitting him in the neck and shoulder. He was put out of commission as I headed his way down the hall.

Down the hall, three room entrances could be seen. The farthest room was used as weapons and ammunitions storage. The next closest was a torture chamber where interrogations are carried out. The closest room is the room where hostages and hostiles are imprisoned. I hoped it would be where the Flauntain's would be located, but as my day was going they were nowhere to be found.

It was at that moment that a female scream could be heard. Yes, your thinking is right. Jocelyn Flauntain let out a yelp as she was jostled into the same Jeep Cherokee they put me in the other day. I ran out of the building all the while heading straight for the jeep. Four terrorists ran after me and I shot them. One by one they fell in a line, like a set of dominos.

Dropping the empty clip, I loaded my M1911A1 pistol with my last seven bullets. Baksuane showed fear in his black eyes as he hid behind the open driver side door. He may be very knowledgeable about weapons and explosive, but a monkey could hit a target with better accuracy than he at anything farther than two car lengths. He unloaded his entire Mac-11 clip and only made me move once to avoid getting hit. While running I turned toward the jeep and dropped to one knee. Firing two shots I shattered the doors window and erased Baksuane from the living.

Grabbing the assault rifle that was close by my feet, I ran to the jeep and yelled at the Flauntain's to get in and get down. They complied without any questions. Seeing the keys, to the handcuffs the Flauntain's were wearing, I picked them up and tossed them to Eric who unlocked the cuffs and we drove off in the already running Jeep.

As we accelerated out of the compound, an army style transport truck screamed its tires as it caught up and followed us. Moments after it caught up, the passenger started firing at us in an attempt to stop our jeep from running. I was a little surprised when Eric Flauntain started telling me about how he was drafted into the Vietnam War in the early 60's. He then asked, emphatically, if he could have the AK-47 I picked up in order to fire back at those that were firing at us.

I gave him the gun and the two extra clips I still had, while I drove to avoid the bullets coming our way. Eric broke the glass of the back window as he started firing back. It was evidently clear that Jocelyn was very scared of what was happening. She buried her face into her lap so that only her brunette hair could be seen.

After firing his first clip, the self-effacing Eric reloaded the rifle and hit pay dirt. His bullets had caused the hood of the enemy truck to become dislodge and it was now covering the entire windshield of the truck. Also, the radiator was discharging a slow white smoke. Next, Eric kept firing at the engine till it sparked and started to catch fire.

The terrorists slammed on the brakes and their vehicle swerved to a stop with the vehicle sideways and taking up the entire road. Eric did just what he said he had done to a Vietcong transport truck during his tour. He shot at the back of the truck until several of his bullets hit the trucks tank igniting the fuel and sending six to ten terrorists and their vehicle into a morgue furnace like ball of fire. I think you would have done that too. We stopped just long enough to make sure no one had survived the blast. No survivors were found so we headed for the US embassy in Amman, the capitol of Jordan. We also dropped the rifle next to the fire so as not to be caught with it.

We drove toward the embassy with very little stops and as night rolled in we slept in the jeep. By mid-day after we left the compound we made it to the embassy. I used my department of defense strings and got the three of us on a flight to the UK followed by a connecting flight to D.C. By the morning of the day we left, the Special Police Force of Jordan arrived to round up the rest of the Chosen Ones members.

When the SPF arrived they found that six of the top ten most important Chosen Ones members were dead. Five of them caught a bullet by my hands and the other was the one shooting at us from the truck. Others in the CIA will try to tell you what the right thing to do is. They will give you scenarios and then try to tell you the right thing you should do if you are ever in that situation. They will remind you that they have been doing this job longer than you and they know what is best for you.

Now if I give you a piece of advice, more than anyone you will ever work with or for, you should take notice and listen well. Not ONE person ever employed by the CIA can give you better advice than I. Just ask yourself, who else in the CIA has taken down an entire organization by himself? You cannot find one agent that has. Yet I took down an organization, may I remind you, that was one of the wealthiest and most connected on the planet.

I KILLED Ominia Romitti a Kulo Kula! I took the Chosen Ones off the map and put them out of commission. No one else can say they have done that to any group or organization! Some of them will even tell you that I am just another agent and that they could do what I have done better than I have done it. If I were you I would look them in the face and tell them that they are the biggest liars you have ever met. There is not a record at the farm I do not have. There is not a test where anyone has scored higher than I.

Now I hate to boast about myself, but there is a group within the CIA that, still to this day, think it is impossible that I could have ever done what I did to the Chosen Ones. They believe that the rival terrorists from the Saudi Arabia/Jordanian border were the ones responsible. I tell you they are full of it because time and again I keep proving that I am the best agent in the entire CIA.

Now I am glad that I took out the Chosen Ones. I just put a big hole in Anna Layata's spy ring. She used the Chosen Ones like most spies use assets. She funded their holy wars and they gave her equipment and passages to places undetected. The way I see it is that if I could not capture her, I would make life for her a living hell by taking away every piece of help she has. I would take away everything, and if need be I was going to get every asset she had to turn on her.

Remember, life can be hell if you double cross the

world. Madam Layata has done that and this was the beginning of me crashing everything down around her. If you cross the world the same things will happen to you too. By taking out the Chosen Ones I sent a message to Miss Layata. The message was clear stating that I am a party crasher and I do not just crash parties, I burn them to the ground.

Venice of the North

Romani Gudenchki, nothing more than an
American spies alias, was created in the late summer of
nineteen eighty-one. The alias of Romani has an alias as an
older brother named Nikolai. A British MI6 agent by the
name of Daniel Macradin is the owner of the alias Nikolai
Gudenchki. I met Daniel while on a mission in a city
known as the Venice of the North. The city of Amsterdam
got that nickname because of its many canals that resemble
those of Venice, Italy.

Until that mission in Amsterdam, I had never met
Daniel. Daniel, I swear, could win a celebrity look-alike
contest because he bears a striking resemblance to Peter
O'Toole from the movie Lawrence of Arabia. If you were
to ask Daniel to describe me, he would say that I look like a
mixture of Sean Connery in Dr. No and Mel Gibson in Mad
Max.

My mission to Amsterdam was very cut and dry. I
was to go to Amsterdam and spy on Andrenie Korinniko,
bring back his handler, and gather information on his
contacts in Western Europe. Does the mission sound easy?
This job is never as easy as it seems, and by now, I thought
you would know that.

The CIA wanted to control Andrenie's flow of information by controlling his handler. They figured if his handler was turned and working for us, that he or she would feed us the real information and present false documents back to Russia. They wanted me to make his handler become my double agent. Now that is a job within a job.

Adam Karzikowski was a brash young agent who had only been in the field for a couple of years. He was a tall dark skinned man with blond hair and blue eyes. He looked like the typical California surfer dude with the body type to match. He was an agent with potential if not for the fact that he thinks more with his genitals than with his brain. He is typical of the type of agent that finds it easier to seduce their opposite sex targets rather than find other ways to turn them. If you did not already know, that is NOT my style. My wife would make my life hell if I were that kind of guy.

They told me that for this mission I was going to work with Adam. I do not mind working with others, but I do my best work when I am alone in the field. Adam is the reason that I follow the philosophy that you should only trust in those you trust in yourself, for trust in anyone else is like signing a death wish. In this job, trust does not come easy and one should not take it lightly. Anybody will try anything to be on top. People constantly change sides for many different reasons. Even ones grandma would stab you in the back if she thought she could get ahead in the game.

Adam and I arrived in Amsterdam because intelligence had told us that Andrenie was going to be holding a spy conference to pass along information, trade routes, blueprints, and even young women that could be turned into spies. Andrenie is the guy who's known as the spy pimp. His nickname comes from the fact that he is a Russian spy who deals in human sexual trafficking as a way of getting information out of potential targets. He runs a prostitution ring out of Amsterdam while owning one eighth of all prostitutes in the red light district. He tries to tell the world that he is just a businessman, but the truth is that he fools no one. He uses his "business" to try to hide his spy craft.

Andrenie just bought a nightclub, near the red light district, named Partij Uw Problemen Weg, which is Dutch for Party Your Trouble Away. Adam and I both knew that the best way to observe Andrenie and to find his handler was to watch him at his club where he partied every night. We did not know that his little conference was going to hold more than just his handler. Even several agents from other agencies were going to show up.

The club was a large dance hall with about ten tables on either side of the room. Every third table had a round couch instead of barstools. The bar covered one whole side of the room and was on the opposite side of the room from the entrance. There had to be a bouncer at least every twenty feet in this place. The bar seated about thirty people and three females were working behind it. Above the bar there is a balcony reserved for the VIP's that come to the club.

At each corner of the room, next to the bar, there was a large stripper's pole where women would dance for tips. Behind the bar were three rooms for private dances and other activities if you catch my drift. Some of you would enjoy this place, while the rest of you would be appalled at the description I am giving you. Next to the "dance pole" on the right is where the two disc jockeys positioned several turntables to play the beats heard throughout the club. I do not know about you but I would prefer to listen to a softer rock style of music. I just finished listening to the new album Escape from Journey that came out last week and every song on it was better than the dance beats this club calls music.

Above the bar was a cage where a dancer could be

raised and lowered while she danced for the boys below. In the club, they call the women dancers, but they are just glorified exotic dancers and strippers for the sinful man's delight. If you ask me, the place is more of a gentleman's club than a nightclub. That is not what they call it though.

The dance floor was the size of half of a professional soccer field. The dance floor had to hold at least one thousand people. The Russians love the place for they can launder money through the bar. This is even a place the Russian mob uses because most governments cannot touch it.

We took a seat at one of the couch tables and Adam went to ogle over the strawberry blond flipping around one of the poles. I bet you think just like me. Thinking that this young brazen kid was going to be involved with some woman and blow our cover. The worst part of this mission is that Adam has been stationed in Amsterdam for just over a year. He probably knows some of the girls in here and he may have already given them information. As I already told you, not many people can be trusted on this job.

I decided while he was getting touchy feely with the blond, I would do some actual surveillance. I ordered a Mai Tai and headed over to the pool tables located back behind one of the poles. I could see Adam was having a good time with his gal, for he just pounded his forth silver bullet shot in his first hour since we got here. Even you can see that Adam was going to be worth nothing to me on this mission.

I shot my first round of pool by myself. After I just about started my second game, a dark blond asked to play me in a game. He asked me a bunch of questions about where to eat and if I knew of any places to visit that one would not find in a travel book. He told me he was just out of the navy and taking a vacation.

Periodically, he would stare, with his bluish green eyes, toward the crowd on the dance floor as if he was looking for someone. After a couple of games, we headed back to my table where Adam and his gal Karin were sitting. The blond told me his name was Danny.

I found it a little odd that Danny kept looking between the entrance and the VIP section. He kept going back and forth as if he was a nervous wreck. Just as he ordered a long island ice tea, a robust man with protruding high cheekbones and dark hair entered the club. Most everyone in the club seemed to acknowledge the man as he made his way to the VIP section of the club.

I overheard the man speak to a bouncer in a thick Russian accent about wanting some beauties to entertain his party guests in the VIP lounge. He also wanted a bottle of the best vodka sent with them. He also mentioned something about having the guards be on the lookout for an American national. I was not sure what that meant, but it was putting me on the lookout too. Was he talking about Adam or me? Your guess is as good as mine is.

After the bouncer left, Andrenie ascended the stairs to the VIP lounge. About twenty minutes after Andrenie went upstairs, a slightly overweight man in a pinstriped suit and a fedora came in with an entourage of women that make the working girls of this club seem like leftover diner garbage, that even alley cats refuse to touch. For a moment, his dark eyes caught mine and even you could see they had a tired look with a killer's instinct.

The American gangster look alike is none other than Findrak Fiendra. Findrak is a world-class smuggler. He was born in Russia, but he works for himself and the highest bidder rather than ally with any one country. He has it in with several different groups, including the Russian mafia. If you need a cover Id, Findrak can make one that is so airtight that even the CIA cannot tell the difference. He is the world's foremost creator of false identities and if it can be smuggled anywhere, he can move it.

From the moment that Andrenie made it to his seat on the balcony, he positioned himself to be looking out over the balcony to be able to watch who comes and goes into the club. Adam was the person supplying the CIA with information on Andrenie and his upcoming conference. He told us that on Friday the conference would convene. Since today was Wednesday night, we had roughly two nights to gather intelligence on those known to be showing up at the "gathering."

Most of the time that is spent in the field consists of gathering information on your target(s). If you are to report on a person, then you may want to note his daily routines. Does the target walk to the same place for coffee every day or do they work at the same building every day? Is there several people coming and going from their place of residence? Is their home well-guarded or is it easy to break into? These are valid questions that must be answered about a subject one is tasked to spy on; and this is the type of information that a field operative will relay back to Langley for further review.

I have already answered some of these questions about Andrenie and the place where the spy meeting was to take place. There is two armed guards standing by the front entrance, one by each dance pole, four in the VIP lounge, two near the door leading to the office, and three guards are walking the floor. That makes thirteen armed guards in the club and even you can assume that each of the spies was going to be armed.

The CIA was informed through chatter that at least five people were going to attend this meeting. Those known going to be in attendance are: Andrenie, Findrak, Andrenie's handler whose identity is unknown, an assassin that is known as Draugr named after the Norse mythological creature of the same name, and another Russian spy named Natalya Arsyevovin whose very good at getting people to become assets for the KGB.

Danny left our table and joined a small group after having only one drink with us. He was a peculiar man whom I had trouble reading, which if you knew me you would also find strange. I can usually read people very well, and like a profiler, I can usually tell a lot about them. To me, Danny was not a young party dude just out of the navy. He seemed more like a man on a mission of which I could not tell what it was.

Around two, I started to become tired so I headed back to my hotel room. When I left Adam, he was still in a high-energy party mode with Karin. Some of you may be just like Adam and can party all night. I can too, but I prefer at least some rest. Rest is a key factor when in the field. A tired agent is a slow agent, and a slow agent is just as good as a dead agent.

I spent most of the next day following Andrenie from his loft to several different places. He had lunch with a couple of Dutch businessmen, and then he picked up his dry cleaning. He then spent a few hours walking the red light district talking to several women. I gather, and I think you would too, that he was obtaining the information that his women gathered from the men they were with over the last few days.

After his talks with his women, Andrenie ordered dinner and spent most of the evening in the company of a dark skinned woman. Around eleven at night, Andrenie went to his club where I went through round two of my observations of the club. This night there was a more rowdy crowd. Two fights broke out and a drunken patron that was taken out back and dealt with, roughed one of the dancers up. I think even you can figure out what that meant.

The night was very uneventful for the most part. I did notice that Ayalah Ronia, a female agent of Mossad, was at the club. Mossad, the Israeli intelligence agency, has their fingers in just about everything you can imagine. It should be no surprise to you as it was not to me that she would be present.

Friday came rolling around and I spent most of the day observing the guards outside the club. Party Your Trouble Away is right next to a bistro and a bar selling this drink that is illegal in the US. If you can get into the VIP lounge whiles in the club, there is an outside balcony that overlooks a canal for boat rides and the bridge built over it. There is even a stairwell leading to a small dock just off the balcony, but to get to it one has to get passed the three guards always standing near the stairs.

Besides the thirteen guards, I noted two days ago, there are two guards outside by the front gate watching people and a bouncer giving or denying access into the club as well as the three guards on the balcony. With the amount of chaos going to be going on during the night, it was not going to be easy to grab Andrenie's handler. Especially, since neither you nor I know what his handler looks like. The thing I hate, and I think you would too, is that to navigate in this club during the big meeting is going to be insane because of the alphabet soup of agencies going to have agents with agenda's on site.

Eight thirty came around and it was time to gather at the club for the party was about to begin. Adam and I gathered at a round table and waited for party members to arrive. Ayalah, whom I caught out of the corner of my eye, was standing at the bar in a pair of leather pants with a dark sports bra and a long sleeved unzipped studded leather jacket that came down to just above her belly. Her black hair was in a ponytail and I could see she had to fight off several men who wanted to buy her drinks while drooling over how she looked. French intelligence had two agents playing pool as the clock struck ten.

At that time, Findrak entered with his usual entourage of women and made his way up to the lounge. This time his suit was deep purple with vertical black stripes and a black fedora. Andrenie was already waiting with a bottle of champagne on ice. Natalya Arsyevovin entered wearing a playful navy blue lace mini skirt cocktail dress. If Draugr had entered, I was unaware for no one can put a face to his or her name. Draugr got that name for leaving bits of Norse mythology, on the creature, near every one of his victims.

At approximately eleven, Andrenie ordered the doors closed and that no one could enter the club. Even though the club was only at half capacity, the guards told the waiting partygoers that the place was full and turned them all away. They then locked the doors so that no person could enter or leave.

Now was the time to either put a plan into action or

let the mission die on the spot. The fact that there was no time to put a plan into action would surprise even you. At near fifteen minutes past the hour, two guards came over to my table and started to talk to Adam's girlfriend Karin. If you remember, Karin is the dance girl he partied with the first night we got to the club. Karin let her blond hair fall flat just covering her shoulders. She wore a white satin bra barely covering up her somewhat large chest and had on a go-go dancer frilly style mini skirt with brown knee high stilettos.

They conversed for a few moments about what she was doing at our table. In addition, they talked about why she did not have her dossier with her. The last thing I heard Andrenie's personal bodyguard mention was something about Karin needing to get upstairs to the "meeting" before Andrenie became enraged. Andrenie is not a patient man and becomes very enraged when things do not go his way. Just hearing their conversation, you would be just like me, I knew things were going to go from joyful to the destruction of Sodom and Gomorrah faster than anyone could have reacted.

Karin got out of her seat, put her drink on the table, and headed toward the stairs leading up to the VIP lounge. Soon as she made it to the top of the stairs, Andrenie ordered three guards to come over to my table and escort us to the meeting upstairs. I had the most puzzled look on my face as several thoughts ran through my brain during which they escorted me upstairs with a gun nudged into my spine. Even you would not try something with all the eyes on you, while having no weapons.

When they seated me on a small couch across from Andrenie and Findrak, my confusion quickly turned to downright fury. Adam started exchanging greeting style hugs with Findrak, Andrenie, and Natalya. He then exchanged kisses on the cheek with Andrenie's handler. His handler was an auburn woman with hazel eyes that pierced my heart. His handler, Madam Layata, is the same woman that left me for dead in Cambodia a few years back.

I KNEW I should not have trusted that MOTHER…! Do you remember my advice on trust? Adam IS the REASON I trust just about NO ONE when I am in the FIELD! My country and I were sold out for women and money because the weasel, Adam Karzikowski, thinks with his genitals and not his brain. Adam had been working for the Russians for the past eight months and had been supplying them with information on CIA operations in and around the Netherlands.

The group as a whole, led by Adam's idea, decided

they were going to send the CIA a message. They thought it would be a good message by sending me back to the CIA in boxes and pieces. For a while, the group talked about different missions going on in Western Europe. Andrenie's working girls told him about businessmen setting up accounts in Zurich to hide millions from the Dutch and French governments. The girls even obtained the bank account numbers and access passwords. The girls, also, had obtained information on where one could steal plans for a high-energy low noise laser that can cut threw concrete as if it were a knife cutting threw warm butter.

Findrak had the Id's he made so that the Russians could get spies undetected into Spain, France, and Scotland. He also had the location of where he had stashed equipment that was to be used to get out one of their spies, with a blown cover, in Canada. They talked for a bit about having Draugr be the one to get the spy out of Canada. Still I had no idea who Draugr really was and Draugr's identity was not mentioned.

While being handcuffed to a chair, all I could do was sit and listen to what they said. After Adam slammed his fist into my abdomen, a few times, they forced me to drink a vodka mixed drink. Moments after I drank it I felt myself getting dizzy just before I passed out.

I woke up tied to a chair without a shirt on. I was in a poorly lit warehouse room that had a pungent and repulsive fishy odor. They had strapped metal bands around my biceps and attached jumper cables to the bands. The cables were attached to a battery from which they could turn on by just a switch. You might be terrified of what is to come but you will learn that in these moments one must remain calm. Some of you will last only a couple of jolts all the while some of you will last half an hour maybe a little more.

After two hours of them trying hard to get me to talk, and with me resisting, they were frustrated. Andrenie had sent Anna to interrogate me while he tended to other business. I spent two hours going round with electricity and Anna when Findrak came into the room. He handed her some kind of thick green liquid in a tall glass. He wanted her to force me to drink it because they needed my energy up if they were to get me to talk.

I can see that you think that by now you would have spilled any information they wanted in hopes of self-preservation. I did not feel like I could hold out much longer. Anna shoved that drink down my throat and I about chucked it all back up. Her next comment was about how I had just one hour to talk and then she would get me medical attention or the cocktail I swallowed would kill me.

At that moment, Anna turned my chair and showed me the dead body of Ayalah Ronia who had been sexually assaulted, beaten and, electrically shocked. I also saw her coat and bra ripped and on the floor. I noticed that since she did not talk, as Anna pointed out, they took a butchers knife and removed her nipples from her chest to send back to Tel Aviv.

Slowly Anna walked over to Ayalah's body and removed her Star of David necklace from around her neck. She then slowly and agonizingly walked back to the table where the battery and switch had been placed. She picked up the switch and put her hand on it, making me sweat thinking she was going to turn it on. WHAM! A noise that knocked Anna out of the chair bounced off the room walls as the wooden doors slammed against the wall.

As the door opened, I noticed the dark blond from the other night at the club. He was holding his left arm around Findrak Findra's throat as he had a gun pointed at his right temple. He was yelling at Anna while instructing her to do what he wanted or she would see Findrak's brain splattered all over the room. Not being armed and not wanting her friend shot, Anna unhooked me from the chair as Findrak came to give me a hand.

The blond with the gun called all the shots in that room, for he was the only one armed. The two of them, with Findrak forced, helped me into the backseat of a car as they took me to a hospital. The doctors pumped my stomach to remove the toxic drink from my body. I was kept overnight for observation, and the blond stayed with me while being handcuffed to Findrak. He convinced the hospital staff that he was a cop, Findrak was his prisoner, and I was his partner.

The next day I was taken out of the hospital and the three of us took a couple hours ride to a house located in a town called Aalsmeer. On the drive, the blond told me a little about himself, and he told me why he came to get me. His real name is Daniel Macradin and he is an agent of MI6 with a license to kill number 0056. He told me to call him Daniel for he hates when anybody calls him anything else. He was sent to Amsterdam to eliminate Andrenie and to put an end to Draugr. MI6 had an agent ready to take command of Andrenie's operation soon as he was eliminated.

Daniel was being given shared information from the CIA to help on his mission to locate Draugr. There is a funny thing about Daniel's information, and I think you can see where this is going. The man supplying Daniel with his intelligence was none other than that RAT Adam Karzikowski who is GOING to EAT a BULLET next time I SEE HIM! When I was taken up to the VIP lounge and Daniel saw that Adam was giving everyone hello hugs he knew I was CIA and in trouble.

He figured that if he could help me out, I would give him a hand in finishing both of our missions. Both missions had already gone to hell thanks to Adam. It is because of Adam that Daniel knew I was a fellow agent form a fellow agency. We stayed at MI6's safe house for a week with me recuperating, and the two of us grilling every little secret Findrak had stored in his brain. It got so creepy because he started talking about his childhood as if we were psychiatrists charging him by the hour.

Over the course of the next ten days, Findrak bargained with us not to kill him. In exchange, he created two of his best quality full proof identities he ever made. From this deal came the identities of Nikolai and Romoni Gudenchki. One was Russian and the other was Ukrainian. Since I learned my Russian from my grandpa's neighbor, who was a Ukrainian refugee and since my dialect was Ukrainian, Romani was from there. Both Nikolai and Romani are brothers who were separated by a divorce where Romani left with his father to live in Ukraine and

Nikolai stayed with his mom in Russia. That is the story Findrak created with the identities. To this day governments think Daniel and I are separate people from the Gudenchki's.

Findrak gave us tons of information on Russian spies in Western Europe, mostly in Netherlands and France. He spilled his guts on Andrenie's warehouse, while telling us of its location and the contents inside. He also told us about ways to cripple the Russian mobs money laundering scheme at the club. Findrak only made us our identities after he told us everything he knew and then thought that we were going to kill him. Instead of killing him, Daniel had him transferred to a prison somewhere in the UK.

It only took the Russian's four days to find Findrak's location. After they found him, they had him executed while he was waiting to be processed by the British government. I also did not get the chance to put a bullet into Adam's skull. He was found floating two miles down the channel from the back of the club. He had his neck broke and a note inside a sandwich bag with a passage about the shepherd, who also had a broken neck, from the Eyrbyggja Saga of the Norse. It turns out that the assassin Draugr was none other than Adam's girlfriend Karin who got him to turn on Daniel and I. Daniel caught up to Karin two years later in Rome and killed her on a botched assassination attempt of the British ambassador to Italy.

Over the course of the next month, with the information we were given, Daniel and I slowly emptied Andrenie's warehouse of every valuable thing within it. Most of the items ended up in the hands of the Dutch government, while some we kept and others we dumped into several channels. Next, we started paying people to spread false information throughout the Red Light District including the false information we spread. We employed the tactic used in Ian Fleming's novel Casino Royale.

The tactic is for Bond to bankrupt Le Chiffre at the baccarat tables and then when his organization had lost all its money the Russian government would eliminate Le Chiffre from the spy game. Our plan was similar. We were going to make Andrenie's network of working girls feed the Russian government so much false information that they would see it as a waste of money and resources while finding no other option but to remove Andrenie from his post in the Netherlands.

Over that month that we went all over Amsterdam spreading all sorts of information and false documents, Andrenie did exactly what we wanted him to do. He took that documents and information, and like a kid with twenty bucks to spend in a toy store, he got all excited thinking he was going to get a huge reward for his ability to gather such sensitive and possibly crippling materials on Russia's enemies. Just like that kid in the store that does not check to see if the toy is defective, Andrenie did not investigate the information and documents because the sources that gave him the intelligence had never failed him before and were always reliable. You could have even noticed that his sources were reliable, that is, until his sources came across the Gudenchki brothers of Daniel Macradin and Joey Scapeotto.

The sad thing for Andrenie is that his club was paid for by money courtesy of the Russian government. I bet you can guess what the Russian's did to Andrenie once all the information was deemed unreliable. Due to our misinformation, the Russians lost six spies, and had just the same number of operations blown. We also uncovered three deep cover moles within allied intelligence agencies in the process of our mission. Daniel completed all but the executing of Draugr and my mission to capture Andrenie's handler, Anna Layata, was a bust. Even so, we had a job well done and we got more out of our missions than we were asked to do. From this mission I met Daniel who is the only man I have ever trusted in the field. You should always remember what I said about trust. It would also not be long before I was back on the trail of one Madam Anna Layata.

The Forbidden City

I can feel it; that you think I am a disgrace to the CIA for taking resources from the Russians. If I am to make them believe that I am one of their operatives named Gudenchki, then I need to take any resources that they are willing to give me. Sometimes I leave their gadgets and equipment in places that make everyone think that a Russian is to blame for whatever just happened, and not an American spy. I am sure that even you would take extra ammunition and gadgets if given to you. It is like saying that your boss would give you more money each year to do your job. You know you would take it.

One year and a few months after I completely dismantled the Chosen Ones, the CIA thought they would send me on a quick get in and get out not so stressful mission. The CIA sent me to make my way from the British territory of Hong Kong to the Forbidden City. I was to bring a Chinese political prisoner out of the country to grant him asylum in the US in exchange for his knowledge on Chinese technology. He wanted asylum because he opposed the Chinese leaders and the way the Peoples Republic was treating it citizens by misusing his work. Not to mention he opposed everything that communist's believe. They were going to throw him in jail and possibly execute him as an example by the Chinese government for defiling them, so time was not going to be my friend.

The CIA wanted no trace of American involvement in the extraction of Chinese political prisoner Kwai Xui. The only comfort that my handler gave to me, Aaron Greetox, was a free passage into the Peoples Republic. There was going to be no gadgets and no weapons on this mission. It was going to be just my brains and me on this extraction. You would think they would give me at least a listening device or something to detect how many people were at the compound where they held Kwai.

Aaron Greetox is a man of few rules. One of them are no collateral damage. A mission is a complete success with little to no collateral damage in his eyes. You can imagine how mad he must have been when I brought the Flauntaine's back from Jordan. Aaron is taller than I am by a few inches, and has a scar under his left eye. He got the scar when stopping a bar dispute as a MP for the marines while in Vietnam in the early part of the US involvement.

Aaron has some of the same opinions as Robert De Nero's character in Taxi Driver. He wears his blond hair as if he was in the service. He keeps his body in shape, and Aaron is built just as Kurt Russell was in Escape from New

York, except for a clean-shaven face and no eye patch. With his oval shaped face, wearing dark sunglasses, he embodies the typical suit wearing spy that I know you all picture when I say government agent.

The one thing that I hate about working for Aaron is that he has his agents regularly check in with him every other day. If one does not check in with Aaron he will either write you off as captured and follow CIA protocol or come looking for you and pull you off the mission no matter how close you may be to finishing. You may find him a little controlling and hard to bear when I tell you he once blew a three-year operation because an agent failed to check in by no more than eight hours. Working for him, you follow his rules or you do not get to be in the field. I am not sure about you, but I think checking in once every two to three days are fine unless the mission is time sensitive.

Aaron and I got on a ferry and snuck into China from Hong Kong. We parted ways in the city of Guangzhou, historically known as Canton. Aaron told me that this was as far as CIA involvement could go, and that the rest of the mission was on me. Seeing that I had absolutely nothing on me except seven thousand Chinese Yuan (renminbi) and a satellite phone, this was not going to be an easy assignment. For those of you who do not know, that is the name of the Chinese currency. The exchange rate is roughly one point five Yuan per dollar.

Using my Russian contacts as Romani Gudenchki, I knew I could get a few things courtesy of the KGB. You might call me disloyal by reaching out to the KGB, but when you have a Russian cover identity, you need to reach out, periodically, to keep it intact. The Russians have a distinctive night vision scope that I hoped to get my hands on. I also needed a weapon, so I reached out to a Communist arms dealer in Shanghai. It took me almost two full days to get from Guangzhou to Shanghai due to my lack of transportation and broken Mandarin.

When I finally met with Vladimir Gauzlik, he gave me a Russian made night vision scope, a Makarov pistol, and a briefcase containing an unassembled Russian Dragunov sniper rifle. If it were up to me, I would be using a M1911A1 pistol and the Marines M40A1 sniper rifle over any Russian weapon on the market. To me, the Makarov pistol is always inaccurate and I have to aim it up and to the left just to get a decent shot. The arms dealer gave me the weapons that he did because I convinced him the Russians wanted me to eliminate Kwai instead of help him get out of the country as I was going to do.

For this assignment, you might think me crazy to use Russian weapons over my countries counterpart. What better way to get the Chinese to think that the Russians helped him escape instead of being allies than to leave Russian weapons that only use Russian made ammunition. See, I am not as stupid as some of you think I am. You know if you could frame a Russian spy on the world stage that you would do it.

Romanov Sulomanik is a Russian spy and hit man. He uses the exact weapons and equipment that I had requested from Vladimir. I hoped to get Kwai out of the compound they kept him in and frame Romanov in the process. It took a little over a day to drive from Shanghai to the Forbidden City. I did so in a crappy beat up vehicle that Vladimir gave me. A few times, I felt the car was going to break down on the side of some road when I was miles from anywhere.

The Forbidden City, the People's Republic of China's capital, is one of the largest and most robust of all cities in this country. In 1406, construction began on the Forbidden Palace, and it was complete in 1420. It consists of between nine hundred and a thousand buildings and was the capital locale of China for centuries. The Forbidden City is now no more than a piece of culture and the civic life of the citizens of Beijing. Tiananmen Square is located to the south of the Forbidden Palace. The buildings are adorned with classical Chinese architecture. Many of the buildings have been painted with Buddhist or Taoist art.

The city has a population of nearly nine point two million people. Beijing buildings have a blend of imperial Chinese architecture and a boxy style that can be seen throughout the country. With the crowdedness of the city, even you could go unnoticed after committing a crime. They kept Kwai prisoner in a compound located in the far eastern part of Beijing's Tongzhou District. I stayed in a hotel in the Chaoyang district of the city. It is the government district of the city. My hotel room was quite small, and for your information, it was no better than a stay at a Motel 6.

All that I knew from CIA intelligence was the location of the compound where the Chinese held Kwai. I geared myself for the next phase of my assignment, surveillance. Is it boring? Some of you might think so and the rest of you might relish in the challenges that it imposes.

I drove my crappy car to the neighborhood in which Kwai was being kept. I parked the car a block over from the compound mansion that the Chinese were using as a makeshift holding cell. The car I was given is so crappy I thought that armed guards would hear me a mile away. If I started the car in front of the White House, you could hear it making noise on the steps of the US Capitol building. The homes in the area looked very upscale and they were close enough together that it looked as if a houses backyard was smaller than some American kitchens. The houses are arranged in a u-shape with a single walkway down the middle leading to the backdoor of every house in the neighborhood.

The biggest house in this neighborhood consisted of a one full block home with a three-foot wall built into the side of a hill that stood taller than the other houses. The house had a beautiful Asian style garden adorned with several types of indigenous trees with a creek built around the house. A two foot arched and raised cobblestone walkway leads from the massive driveway to the front door of the house, which stands two stories high in the back half and one story in the front half. The house itself had an imperial architectural style with bright red bricks and yellow and brown colors on the rooftops. I bet you are wondering what kind of person could afford to live in a place as big as this. So was I.

I climbed up to the top of the hill and positioned

myself so that I was looking down into the compound. I started to take pictures with the high-powered camera that I just bought at an expensive tourist shop. Now here comes the daunting task of taking photographs of the people coming and going in and out of the compound.

During surveillance, one key thing to look for is security. Questions that need answering could be any or all the following: How many guards are present? Are they armed and if so with what are they armed? Do the guards work on a schedule? Is it by shifts? Do they patrol a designated area? Do they stay in one place at all times? What is your access to the building in which you need to enter? How many people are coming and going?

Once you have answered these questions, you can begin to devise a plan and start to put it into action. Strength in many bodies will win a gun battle but strength in many minds will complete a mission. Remember that you can execute a well thought out plan to perfection no matter how many people are standing in opposition as long as you stay cool and stay one-step ahead of your enemy.

I spent most of the day watching guards who worked a six-hour shift. Each guard carried with them an AK-47 or an Uzi. A few of China's military officers came to the compound and I could see them assaulting a man tied to a chair on the second floor of the house. Every couple of hours a young maiden would come into the room to tend to the tied man's wounds and to give him a drink or two. After several hours of what looked like an interrogation, the military and government officials left as the day turned into night.

I decided that I would come back the next day to watch and see if anything changed from day to day. I woke up early in the morning, before sunrise, and had my photos developed as I ate breakfast at a marketplace restaurant. It took roughly one hour to get my pictures developed. I then spent the next two hours going over the pictures as I devised my plan. For you information, the photos consisted of seven guards, officers, license plates, and the best shots of the house I could get.

The stairs leading to the second floor is not very wide and they are steep as they spiral between levels of the house. The walls of the second floor is made entirely of panes of window glass similar to a high-rise office building. From what I could gather, the upstairs looked like a studio apartment, in terms of its layout.

Should I create a distraction and sneak my way in or should I just walk onto the compound with bullets ablaze? Quick decisions like this are all too common when in the field. If you are like me, and you know if you are, then you will go over every possible outcome until the moment you make that final decision.

From my hotel room I did my usual report back to Aaron, and he told me that on orders from above his pay grade, I was to wait further instructions as I continue to monitor the situation. The CIA, as Aaron told me, was sending a group of three highly trained black ops agents to aid me in the extraction and that I was to wait until they arrived in a day or two. Once a marine always a marine and like a good one I tried to follow the orders given to me. Even you would follow what your boss says if you want to stay in the field.

I went back to the same spot I had been at the day before and watched a different scene unfold. The compound had double the number of guards as it did yesterday and there were more people in the house. It got ugly at midday when the fourth car pulled into the compound. A dark haired woman with a dancer's body and a bosom that rivals Dolly Parton got out of the car. She could not have been any taller than Michael J. Fox could and her body language showed that she was not happy being summoned to the compound. She had on a black jogging suit with pinkish purple stripes down the sides. I quickly recognized her as a Russian interrogator and spy named Aziha Moniva, a member of Madam Layata's ring of spies.

If you know anything about me and my encounters with Russian spies, than you know this cannot be a good situation for me. Like the calm minded person that I am, I pulled out my scope and kept watch on every move Aziha made. She entered the house and two Chinese fellows greeted her. They sat and talked with her on the couches near the stairs. After a half of an hour of watching the three of them chat on the couch, a short muscular fellow entered my view and showed Aziha a construction workers toolbox.

After moments of looking in the toolbox, Aziha and the muscular fellow followed the other two men upstairs to the room where they had been keeping Kwai. Soon as they got upstairs, I could see Aziha grab what looked like either hedge clippers or bolt cutters.

If I wanted to save Kwai, I had to act now. I could not wait for the extraction team to get to Beijing. Even you know you would have no choice but to act, and you know I am right for doing so. I put on a pair of gloves and opened the large briefcase I had carried with me. I assembled the Dragunov sniper rifle that was inside and loaded the first of my two ten round clips as I attached the scope to the top of the barrel.

I took a shot at the glass window on the second floor, and with the silencer on the gun, it made a minute noise. The bullet made more noise as it shattered one of the glass panes. I made sure I completely missed everyone on the second floor because I just wanted to scare the crap out of everyone's mind. Panic was going to be my best friend and I think you can see why.

Next, I peppered one of the middle cars in the line of vehicles on the property, firing three shots at its gas tank. I watched as the car lit up like an Independence Day fireworks show. A large ball of flames lifted into the air as every guard hit the ground, not knowing what I was going to do next.

I started doing exactly what the Vietnam War taught me. Either you kill the opposition or they eliminate you. As several of the guards got off the ground to see where my shots originated form, I gave them a coup de main. One by one, my bullets dropped them to their grave as I emptied my first clip. Before they really knew what hit them, half the guards were dead with two guards shot by the same bullet.

The rest of the guards started firing at my position

as they climbed up the hill. To no avail to the remaining guards, I was not where they thought I would be. Remember that you need to stay one-step ahead of the enemy or it is like a chess game and goodbye to your king with checkmate. By the time they got to the top of the hill, I was using a big old tree to climb over the left wall similar to a Hollywood stuntman.

When I got up from my shoulder roll, which I used to avoid broken bones, I grabbed two of the dead guards Uzi's as well as an extra clip for each gun. Sixty four bullets for each Uzi, ten rounds for my strapped Dragunov, and three eight round magazines for the Makarov pistol at my side set me up right where I wanted to be.

At this time, three armed goons came out of the house, and you know they were looking to shoot now and ask later. As they crossed the stone bridge and entered the compound square, they looked astounded when they did not see their intruder. I hid under the bridge in the moat, crouching in two to three feet of water. You would have done the same thing in my position. Go ahead and call me the troll form under the bridge, just like the one in the children's fairytale with the goats. I know you are thinking it.

Placing both sub-machine guns on the bridge, I

surprised the first of the three goons when I put my belt around his neck and choked him until he passed out. I did not kill the man because as I turned toward his friends they tried to shoot me to let him go. Instead, they put several bullets into the passed out man's chest. I then, calmly, put a bullet in each of the two men's skull and put my belt back on.

Grabbing the two guns, I fired them in the direction of the guards coming down the hill in an attempt to keep them at bay. I then entered the house and slammed a chair behind and under the door handle to keep them out for a while. Immediately a buff dude swinging his arms in some kind of kung fu motion greeted me.

He came at me with a high jump kick, which missed. He then tried to swing at me as I dodged and slammed a gun into his ribs like a blunt object. He bent over to catch his breath and instead got the back of the gun in the back of his skull. He hit the ground and my foot hit his face twice as he lay there indefinitely. A cracked rib and a bruised head shall do that to you.

Right as I stopped hitting the man, four armed personnel came charging into the room yelling at me in Mandarin. From what I gathered and from the tone of their voice, I figured they wanted me to put down my weapons and surrender. I did what some of you think I should do. I emptied both machine guns, killing them all. I reloaded as I took a right and entered the kitchen.

The kitchen was very small for there was just enough room for a refrigerator, sink, and stove. The backend of the kitchen led into the dining area with a wooden table able to seat at least ten. Taking a left out of the dining area leads to a couch sitting near the stairs to the second floor. There is also a huge sliding glass door leading to a patio and the rest of the huge Asian style garden. Greeting me down the stairs were the men I saw sitting on the couch with Aziha.

Bullets flew in my direction as I dove behind the couch. I laid on the ground as they shot entire AK-47 clips in my direction. The glass from the door broke and shattered all over the floor and me. When I heard the clicks of both of their guns I stood up and open fired on them and hitting them with multiple bullets to the chest, stomach, and legs. I removed a clip from each sub-machine gun I had and tossed them onto the patio as I pulled out my Dragunov.

I shot several of the guards as they entered through the broken patio door. Then I aimed my gun at the front door as I watched the remaining guards break open the jammed door. I emptied the rest of my rifle as the last of the guards entered the house. Pulling out my pistol, I finished of the rest of the guards as they entered the house, leaving only Aziha and myself to fight.

Soon as I made it up to the top of the stairs, Aziha greeted me with a foot into my chest that sent me to the floor after falling over an ottoman. For a few moments, we exchanged swinging blows until I slammed her head into a bookcase, temporarily halting her assault. I grabbed Kwai and we slowly left the house. We hopped into one of the cars left on the lot, a Honda Quintet, which I had to hot wire to start. I decided to leave my crappy car where I parked it because this car was quieter and in better condition.

I got a minute's head start, but it did not matter. I had to hot-wire the car, which slowed us down a few moments. It was enough time for Aziha to get up and chase us out the building. As we headed north, our escape was not going to be at all easy. Following us was a very angry woman with a sub-machine gun and two pistols all the while riding a motorcycle that someone parked on the side of the house.

We took a right onto a major road and a truck full of goons took a quick U-turn and started speeding up toward us. The three in the cab of the truck seemed aggravated at us as they fired their guns at us. We have the now dead guards of the compound to thank for this truckload of backup to be chasing us. They were the ones that called for them to come and assist at the compound.

It was at this point I thought I would try to ask Kwai why a truckload of goons wanted to shoot out my tires. Kwai explained to me who they were and why they wanted him dead or alive. This was the moment that even you would realize that somebody screwed over somebody in the chain of information by forgetting to mention that not only did the Chinese government want to keep Kwai quiet, so did the Russians and another group lead by Chow Wong, supposed but unconfirmed leader of the local branch of the Sun Yee On. If you do not know, the Sun Yee On is the largest of the Chinese Triads, equivalent of the Japanese Yakuza.

Some of the technology that Kwai promised to share with the US came to China courtesy of the Russian government. This explains why Aziha had interest in Kwai at the compound and why she is in a bitter mood with Kwai and me getting away. You might have been made too if Aziha were you.

To make matters worse, Kwai owes the Triad roughly one million US dollars in gambling debts and he told about his girlfriend. Not only was she three months along with carrying his child and he would not leave without her; she used to be Chow's girl that he brought to China as part of his human trafficking ring. Her name is Maria Josephina Hernada and Chow took her, and forced her to be his girl, from her village just outside Caracas, Venezuela. Kwai took her away from being Chow's slave and the two became inseparable lovers.

I kept the car bobbing and weaving in and out of traffic, but Aziha and the truck kept on my heels. I decided to hop onto the other lane and drive straight at oncoming traffic. Cars were sliding everywhere with drivers crashing into one another trying to avoid a head on ram with my car or the bullets flying at it. After about one mile of driving two more motorcycles, each with two riders, joined the parade of angry triad members wanting me dead. Each motorcycle had a driver and a gunner on the back shooting at this car as well as the truck.

Up ahead I saw an opportunity that only the boldest and daring of you would even think of taking. I put the pedal to the floor of the car and got it screaming at just over one hundred miles per hour. With very few cars in the way, what I did could have gotten me killed and you may only see this done by stunt drivers.

I let off the gas and slammed on the emergency brake as I turned the wheel all the way to the left. Soon as the car started spinning, I let go of the brake and while straightening the wheel I hit the gas. The car spun around more than one hundred and eighty but less than two hundred and seventy degrees before I gained control of it.

To avoid a head on collision, one motorcycle turned to the right and drove into the ditch. This sent their bike high into the air and when they came down, they became hit head on by a truck in the other lane of traffic. Now comes the part that I hate most about car chases, congested city driving with very little room to maneuver a compact vehicle.

Soon as the car stopped squealing, I drove down a small side street. Anyone could see that an advisory would be to drive no more than one car down the street. Two vehicles side by side would not fit down this road. Only a bicycle might fit next to a car driving down this tiny road.

Each building, on the sides of this road, was a factory which was about to let its employees go home for the night. On the right, the factory was full of people making garments and fabrics used to make clothing sold on the international market. My answer to the question you are thinking, I am not sure if it was a sweatshop but I would not be surprised if it was. The other building was a warehouse used for storing and preparing fish for sale in the market place or shipped to restaurants in the nearby area.

I took a hard ninety degree right at the end of the factory and headed straight toward the market place. Aziha and the other motorcycle were right on my heels with the truck lagging a bit behind. Heading straight down the main stretch of road and going about forty miles per hour, I slammed on the brakes and opened my door. Aziha slammed into my open door, which sent her sailing into the air.

When she hit the ground, it looked as if she may have fractured or broken her back. If not, then she had some broken bones. Her bike was a mangled heap of twisted metal that was no longer drivable. Aziha would not be a factor for the rest of our escape. My car door was bent all the way toward the hood of the car and unable to close.

I took to the left and drove down the middle of the fish market scattering people everywhere as I still had a motorcycle and a truck after me. You would do the same and you know it. I slowed down as I turned the corner and told Kwai to get out. He got out and entered a teashop just seconds before the motorcycle turned the corner. The Triad was still chasing me in the car as if they had no idea that Kwai had gotten out.

Soon as I got a little opening, I spun the car around and drove straight at the Triad. Before they could turn around and catch up, I turned another corner and floored the gas. When the car got as fast as it would go, I jumped out and into a pile of full trash bags. Immediately, I got up and started climbing an apartment fire escape.

I waited as my pursuers drove passed me and toward the car. They looked infuriated as they noticed no one was in the car. They turned around and came back my way in search of where I may have gone. From the second story balcony, I shot the gunner on the motorcycle with my pistol. With a shot in the head, the gunner fell off the bike and to the ground. You know that was the right play.

Sliding down the ladder, I watched, as the biker stopped and grabbed his dead friend's gun. He then came down the alley to find me. I was waiting behind a garbage can and as he came down the alley, I struck him with a large piece of wood in the legs. Hitting the ground, I proceeded to put a bullet into his chest. I grabbed his gun and emptied the entire clip, firing it at the truck. I got on the motorcycle as the truck started up again. What did you think I was going to do?

I could see the man in the passenger seat kick the windshield out as I had riddled it with bullet holes. They chased me down, but I knew that this time everything was in my favor. First, I was on a motorcycle that could get into places a truck could not and it has easier mobility. Second, they were no longer shooting at me. Guess they ran out of ammunition.

I thought that I might have some fun with these clowns. I drove circles around them a couple of times and they looked aggravated, as they knew not what to do. One of them got out of the cab of the pickup and he looked as if he was trying to time my passing. I think he wanted to roundhouse kick me right of the bike. He was an average looking goon who was not in a good mood. His first kick missed but not by much. I turned the bike around and went at him just as he wanted.

I popped the bike onto one wheel and drove right at him. The front tire came down right on his stomach and I drove over his face like a speed bump. I loaded my second pistol clip and fired once at the truck. This got them to turn the truck around and move. Not wanting to be shot they went into primal instincts and started to run. I bet you would do the same.

I did something next that under any other

circumstance I would never do. I sped up the bike so I could get it next to the side of the truck. I then pulled my right foot over to the left side of the bike as I kept my hands on the throttle. Next, I jumped off the bike and caught the side of the truck with both hands.

One goon tried to hit my hands and knock me off the side of the truck. I took my gun out of my belt, and while holding on with one hand, I shot the man in the stomach. This sent him backward falling into the other man on the truck. Using all my strength, I climbed into the back of the truck where the other goon tried to shove me off the truck.

The driver started swerving the truck to catch me off balance so I would fall off the truck. I do not think he cared if his friend fell of the truck so long as I went with him. A luck knee to the groin and a solid punch to the face sent the last of the Triad members out of the back of the truck.

The goon sitting next to the driver turned in his seat and started to fire his gun out the back window at me. Of course, I hid on the bed of the truck and waited for him to finish firing. How stupid did he think I would be? I used the butt of the pistol to strike the passenger in the head, knocking him out. I then leaned over and opened the door whiles I grabbed the limp body, pulling him out of the truck. I then swung around into the now vacant spot and pulled my gun on the driver. Kicking him out of the truck, I drove back to the teashop and picked up Kwai.

Kwai was an average looking Chinese man in terms of height and weight. He wore a torn shirt and tattered jeans. It was easy to see the scars on his face from the beatings the Triad and other officials had given to him. Kwai has a rounded face with boney high cheeks and deep black eyes. I could see that his left hand had a few broken fingers. We went to my hotel room for the night to get rest. We were tired and you would be too. I was sore but not sore enough to complain. It comes with the job and you will learn this in time. Kwai took the bed and I slept on the couch.

At four in the morning, I awoke to see no one in the bed. The lights were off and the sun had not come up yet. I raced to get dressed and I opened the room door to a flickering hallway light. I could hear footsteps in the distance and a voice cried out. I ran back into my room, grabbed my gun, and ran after the noises while seeing two leather jacket wearing men shoving Kwai into a silver sedan.

I dove over the second story balcony, hit the hood

of a car and rolled off, and started the pickup as I pulled out after the sedan. What else was I to do? See, even you cannot come up with anything. Chasing the car I only had one thing in mind. Get Kwai safely out of that sedan. They had a minute's head start and I could barely see them on the horizon.

I was going to catch hell from Aaron but at this point, I do not care. My mission was clear and simple: get Kwai out of China safely. At this point, I did not care what was going to happen to me because my only concern was the safety of the prisoner in that silver sedan.

I am not sure if the driver of the car knew I was following because they were not driving all that fast. Guess they figured that I did not see them leave the hotel parking lot. We were driving on a low traffic downtown street. Soon as I caught up to the sedan, I hit the back of the car with the grill of the truck. The car started to swerve so I hit it again. This time the car spun around and came to a screeching halt.

I stopped the truck and got out shooting out one tire on the car. I then walked to the car with my gun pointed at the driver. I opened the back door of the car and allowed Kwai to get out. I punched out one man in the front seat and held the gun on the other.

By this point, I was starting to feel spent. I was feeling done with this place. I was ready to leave China and not care if I ever came back. I drove Kwai to his loft and then walked into a club across the street. I filled Aaron in on all the day's events. To no one's surprise, not even yours, he was in an irate mood because I did not wait for the extraction team to arrive. I tried to explain that I had to react or the Triad may have had Kwai killed.

Aaron reiterated that consequence would ensue from not obeying direct orders and waiting for the team to arrive. I told you that he easily is hot tempered and that he hates collateral damage. Collateral damage, as a black ops agent, comes with the nature of the job. As one who works alone, the damage helps give the appearance that there is more people on my team than there really is. Just like everyone else, I hate the political ramifications but there are times when one has to do things without regard to the outcome.

Right after I hung up the phone, I went over to Kwai's loft and we threw his things under his seat in the truck. Next, we left for the place where his girl, Maria Josephina, was hiding and waiting for Kwai to come get her.

Kwai wanted to meet her at midmorning for he was

tired and wanted to get some rest. My comments were for him to rest in the truck because I was not going to spend another moment in this death-ridden Forbidden City. I was not going to stay in one place for long for I did not want the Triad to find my location. I had had enough of people shooting at me for one day. Even you would feel the same.

Of course, like the rest of this mission, she was not in the apartment that Kwai had her hiding. I searched the whole place and did not see signs of a struggle. I was not sure what to think, but my mind kept thinking that if Kwai was running me around I would leave him for the Triad to find. Someone had made her bed, and the shower was still a little wet suggesting that someone had been here within the hour.

Kwai told me to drive across town to a restaurant called Chow's Chow. Chow's Chow was the place where Maria Josephina used to work. It was where the two had met and the place where Kwai knew he had to get her away from Chow. Oh how I hoped she would be there. In my position, you would have too. I had thirty-six hours to get Kwai and myself to Shanghai where a Japanese boat would be taking us to Tokyo and sneaking us out of China. I so wanted Kwai and his girl united as we left China, but I was prepared to drag Kwai's body to that boat alone and at all cost if need be.

We pulled up to the restaurant and it smelled like a mixture of rice and fish. It looked like something out of a Bruce Lee film and felt more like a Shaolin temple than a place to eat. Inside there were tables with colorful cloths that had an ancient Chinese art on them. At the front, near the door, was a podium where a person would greet and seat customers. In the back was a counter where they took you order and gave it to the cooks to prepare the food.

The owner covered the walls with kung fu weapons and tapestries that had large Chinese proverbs and Taoist wisdom. The tables were round in the middle of the room and square up against the walls. A row of six tables sat against the walls while two rows of five tables were in the middle of the room. I got a bad feeling walking into the place. It was the same type of feeling that you get when you walk into a restaurant that you know is a front for the Italian mob.

There seemed to be a lot of room in the back of the place behind the two swinging doors leading to the kitchen. It also seemed as if nobody was working in the entire place. After a minute or two of waiting and thinking it was time to leave, a very small older Chinese woman came out of the back and asked us to take a seat so she could take our order.

She was very small, only coming up to the middle of my ribs with dark hair that looked longer than her legs. She walked slower than snow falling and spoke with a voice so thick even Kwai had a hard time understanding her Mandarin.

I felt in no mood for food, but not eating in over twelve hours made me stay and place an order of Mongolian chicken while Kwai ate sushi. About thirty minutes after we ordered the short woman served us our meal. Twenty minutes into eating, there was a loud sound of someone dropping an armful of cooking pans. A woman screaming followed it. Even you would know that we were in the right place. How many women do you know that would be in China screaming in Spanish in the back of a random Chinese restaurant?

Soon as the screaming stopped, we could see through the opening in the back wall between the counter and the kitchen. There was a man dragging a woman whiles holding her with his arms across her chest. Kwai stood up and I had to yank his arm because he was about to yell at the goons. The good news was that we were in the right place. The bad news was that the goons were aware of where we were because Kwai had made noise hitting the table and Maria Josephina had cried out to Kwai to help her.

The man holding Maria Josephina said something to a group of men who came through the swinging doors and charged right after me. They each grabbed weapons off the wall and came after me. One grabbed a staff, another grabbed two nunchakus, and the third grabbed a pudoa. A pudoa is a three feet long pole like handle with a two to three feet long curved blade at the end.

I yelled at Kwai to take my pistol and go after Maria Josephina while I grabbed the only weapon I knew how to use, the tonfa. I grabbed them because they are exactly like a police club, which I knew how to use. These three goons just gave me another reason why I hated being in this forsaken country. The goon with the staff started swinging it around above his head and Mr. Nunchaku started spinning them as he moved toward me.

I do not know about you, but I was having a bad feeling about this. Oh how I thought for a moment about jumping out the window and making a run for it. Looking back, I think I should have. Mr. Nunchaku had his hair longer than my wife, who wears her hair just below her underarm. He came at me, swinging both his nunchaku.

I hit the ground onto my belly just as if someone had shot into the restaurant. I got to my knees and drove one club into his mid-section. I drove the end of the other club into his chin. Next, I hit him harder than I had ever hit anyone in my life. I slammed a club into the side of his right knee and throughout the restaurant; you could hear his bones shatter as he hit the ground screaming. His kneecap was all the way facing his left leg and the top of his femur bone had totally broken through the skin and was poking out.

As you can see, I was in no mood to mess around with these goons. You would feel the same way if you were I and you know it. The other two, fully enraged at this point, tried to come at me from both sides and corner me. When they both lunged at me, I rolled over a table to create space. My goal was to keep one of the two in front of the other at all times in the hopes I could turn this fight into a one-on-one instead of two versus one.

The man with the staff had scars covering his body and giving the impression that he enjoys a good fight. Both of the men were shorter than I was. The bladed fellow jumped onto a table and thrust his weapon toward my face. I side stepped his attack and used a club to hit the top of his blade. In doing so, his blade stuck into the table forcing him to take a couple of seconds to pull it out of the wood.

This allowed my time to shove a chair at the other

goon, who stopped it with his foot. He shoved the chair back at me, and with a running start, I jumped over the chair and threw a club at his face. Why would I throw it you ask? I almost cracked the club in half thanks to the broken knee. He swung at me with the staff and I blocked it as I shoved my foot into his chest. Being honest, I would have preferred this was a boxing match rather than a kung fu fight.

He came running at me with his staff and I ducked, shoving my shoulders into his mid-section. I stood up, and like a professional wrestler, I threw him over my shoulder and onto the hardwood floor. Upon standing up, I had to dodge a swinging pudoa. I kicked the table over, knocking the man to the floor, while following that up with a club strike to the other man's face.

The third goon got up after falling and threw a piece of a broken chair at me. He jumped at me, swinging his blade over his head toward the ground. Like a baseball bat, he then tried to swing at my heart. I backed away, tripped over a chair, and saw what I could not believe. The man with the staff was getting up as the bladed weapon swung toward my body. The pudoa missed me but the backswing caught the other man and slit open his left carotid artery.

I dodged the blade as I grabbed the staff and ran

into the kitchen. I noticed the kitchen was empty but still turned on was the griddle in the back of the room. After a minute or two of exchanging and blocking blows, I parried his pudoa. I hit him in the back of the head with the staff, swung my body behind him, and used all my weight and the staff to shove the side of his head onto the griddle.

I held his skull on the griddle until I counted to seven and his face looked worse than any drawing of Batman's enemy Two-Face. With that, I walked outside to look for Kwai and to get out of this forsaken place. To my dismay, the truck was gone and Kwai was nowhere in sight. I am not sure about you, but I was ready to leave this place without Kwai. I was running out of time to get to the boat and not sure that I wanted to wait any longer.

I started looking at options. Up and down, the street was a few cars parked and people were walking by. While I was in the kitchen making a burnt pancake with the goons face, a customer came in and on seeing the carnage, called the police. I could hear their sirens in the distance and they were getting closer. The Chinese government would rather crucify me than trade me back to the US.

Right as I saw the first police vehicle pull up to Chow's Chow, I heard a voice in the distance yelling at me to get in the back and to do it fast. I do not know how it happened and neither you nor I really need to know, but Kwai was hanging out the side of the truck window yelling at me with Maria Josephina sitting next to him.

Finally, things were going right for the first time on this mission. To think that this was supposed to be a simple snatch and grab. I am sure you can hear the relief in my voice as we grabbed a jumbo suitcase full of Maria Josephina's things and drove straight to Shanghai.

On our way out of the city, another car full of Triad members were hot on our trail. I asked Kwai to slow down and I emptied the last four bullets I had into the driver's side window. The car hit the ditch and rolled four or five times before coming to a complete stop. Thankfully, that was the last hitch until we got onto the boat. We made it to the docks with less than an hour to spare. I gave the keys to our contact and told him to keep the truck. From there we made it to Tokyo and then it was home sweet home.

Athens of the North

Over the past couple of years, I have done things while in the field that has caused a few international and political incidents. To those that make the decisions within the CIA, it does not matter that I have gotten the job done and I have done exactly what they wanted me to do. I successfully finished every mission getting all my targets out unharmed and not hospitalized. To those in charge, the game is only political and they want their agents to be politicians and bureaucrats. They want us to take our missions as if we are bridging political wounds.

Over the past couple, years I have inadvertently helped the Chinese government wipe out a huge chunk of the largest Triad and I single handedly dismantled one of the Middle East's biggest and most powerful terrorist organization. For that, they gave me a six-month desk job and six month vacation at half pay because I cause too many political incidents.

They tell me to get the job done at all costs and then they reward me with the phrase: the agency is benching you for your actions. Yet they hired me to do the jobs that no one wants to or can complete. If you were in my shoes right now, you would feel the same as I do right now.

The first half of nineteen eighty-five I spent sitting at a desk sifting through and verifying classified intelligence. The job was something I have not done for long periods in over eight plus years. I have done the job as needed for missions but not day in and day out like this for six months straight.

As of the beginning of the summer, I took my vacation and I took it with my wife Athena. We went to the Athens of the North, Edinburgh Scotland. We chose the Scottish capital because my wife was doing research for a book she was co-writing with a medieval archaeology professor and colleague. For those of you who do not know, my wife is an architectural and art history professor at Georgetown University. She specializes in ancient Greek and medieval religious art and architecture.

My wife went to Edinburgh with three of her students to study a newly discovered remnant of an early medieval Gaelic style church found in the outermost part of the old town district. While my wife worked in the day, I took the time to enjoy the city. At night, we spent time together enjoying the nightlife. It was a well-needed vacation and I am glad I took it with my wife, the most beautiful woman I know.

On our first night of the second month that we had

been in Edinburgh, Athena and I went to a Meadowbank
Thistle versus Albion Rovers football game. While
Athena's students studied and enjoyed the nightlife, we
enjoyed each other's company knowing that in five to six
months we would be parents to out first-born child. We
both decided not to learn the sex of our child until s/he is
born. An even bigger surprise came earlier in the night
when a dark blonde-haired male met me in the lobby as I
was waiting for my wife to come downstairs after her
shower.

     I do not know how Daniel Macradin knew I was in
Scotland or which hotel I was staying at but he found me. I
assumed that our wives had been in contact and that was
how he found me. He told me that he too was on a small
vacation with his wife, Amelia. The four of us went to the
game and afterwards we headed off to dinner at a Scottish
pub where a famous local band, Little Honda, was playing.
All of the world's trouble seemed to disappear and even
you would have felt the same. Even you would have
enjoyed yourself until two drunks started a bar room brawl
that cleared the pub.

     We went back to our hotel to change and headed to
a salsa dance hall for the night was still young. Athena's
sleek and sequined purple cocktail dress glistened in the

moonlight as we walked to the club. Her naturally wavy brunette hair lies just past her shoulders and playfully covered her ears. Her small hoop oval shaped earrings shined in the dance halls light. Her dress hugged her curves in all the right places. Her brown eyes gleamed as she gracefully moved on the dance floor. I am only a few inches taller than she is but she seemed taller in her heels.

Amelia had on a yellow blouse with a black and pink flamenco skirt. She put her red hair into a braided ponytail. I have no idea how she danced in four-inch heels, but she made it look easy. Both Dan and I had on flashy bright tops and loose dress pants. His top was blue, and mine was red. He gave me a little sarcastic attitude because I knew how to salsa better than he did.

Outside the club, there were two street performers vying for the title of best magician. One of them used fire and swords to be impressive while the other used traditional Houdini style magic to show his prowess. Down the street, one could find any number of pubs or late night eateries serving fish and chips. The buildings had the design of a pre nineteen hundreds style seen all over the United Kingdom. The dance hall we were in became a shelter from German bombing during the Great War and converted in the fifties to a dance hall by a Scottish dancer and his Spanish wife.

This neighborhood consisted of narrow streets that are hard to navigate like many old villages in Europe. The buildings, built next to one another, are one to two stories high. Some consist of shops while others are homes. Some of the homes are two flats, split with one apartment upstairs and the other downstairs. Up on the western hill one can drive down a dirt road to a monastery complex with a fifteenth century chapel that is still in use. One could see Edinburgh castle off in the distance if not for the darkness and fog.

The night was calm, quiet, and until now, it was without incident. I should have been more alert and I should have expected something to happen. If I have told you one thing, it is that an agent always needs to expect the unexpected. I guess having time off and being with Athena, who was looking more beautiful than ever, got me to drop my guard more than I am comfortable with doing. If you were in my position, you would have dropped your guard as well and you know it.

I should have remembered what my grandpa always told me. He used to remind me that life is like the seashore, which is either calm or rocky, but it cannot be both at the same time and one should expect a hurricane if the shore has been calm to long. That is some good advice and I want you to remember that.

After about one hour or more of dancing and having a few drinks, I began to get a chill in my lower back which should have been my second clue of oncoming trouble. Dan and I tried to stop to grab a drink and take a quick dance break but the girls would have none of it with the theme to Carman starting to play. Partway through the song, two gentlemen asked if they could cut in for a song or two. Neither of us objected since we wanted a break anyway. This should have been the final clue.

The girls finished Carmen and continued to dance into the next song as we shared information on past cases. Near the end of the song, Dan and I heard what we never wanted to hear. A voice yelled aloud, calling for the Gudenchki brothers to show their faces, and that his actions were our payment for what we have done. He was yelling that we were going to suffer for our past actions.

It was at this time two oversized men grabbed Amelia and forced her outside and into a brown cargo van. At the same time, the man dancing with Athena dropped a gun from under his sleeve and put two bullets into her right chest and one into her left femoral artery.

For a moment, I went completely blind. I could see

nothing but my wife bleeding in front of me. In my position, most of you would feel the same. What I should have done was clothesline the shooter wrestling style right to the ground and then beat the crap out of him. At the same time, Daniel ran out and after his wife. The only good it did him was that he got the license plate number of the van that drove off with his wife.

Everyone in the dance hall made a mad dash toward the exits. At the same time, the bartender called for an ambulance. I took off my shirt and wrapped it around my wife's leg to slow down the bleeding. Without hesitation, Daniel came back into the dance hall and went right for the phone. He called MI5, asking to speak to agent KT of the counter terrorism division. KT stood for Keith Tornell. He told Keith everything that had happened and that the man behind it all was Pavel Korinniko, brother of Andrenie.

Daniel stayed and coordinated with local authorities. They had all access roads out of the city blocked and all trains, planes, and boats monitored for Pavel and Daniel's wife Amelia. At the same time, I went to the hospital with Athena where I stayed for over an hour before I went back to my hotel. I gathered my wife's three students in the lobby and filled them in on their teacher's condition. I also told them to continue to conduct their research as if nothing had happened for I knew Athena would want it that way.

About five in the morning, Daniel met me in the hotel lobby were the hospital told him I would be. We decided to catch some sleep before we met with Keith, who said he would be at the club around two in the afternoon. All I could do is lie in bed and pray that Athena and the baby would be all right. What I wanted to do was grab a couple assault rifles, a few sub-machine guns, a loaded shotgun, and a pistol at my side. I then wanted to walk right into KGB headquarters and shoot anything that by god moves. That is how angry I was but instead I got three hours of sleep.

The lobby clerk, who woke me up, told me that the hospital had called and that my wife was out of surgery. The hospital informed me that she and the baby was in stable but critical condition and not totally in the clear. All signs pointed to the baby being healthy and ok but only time would tell.

As you can tell, I was not happy and I do not think you would be either. I do not mind if they wanted me dead or wanted to take out my friends, but they should have NEVER MESSED WITH MY FAMILY! If they knew what was best for their life, they NEVER would have

SHOT MY WIFE! I got some good advice that both you and they should take. If you want to eliminate someone, then put a bullet between his or her eyes. If you want to anger someone, target his or her family.

NOW if you REALLY want to mess with someone, you take away everything he or she holds near to his or her heart! Take away every security they have. Leave them with no income, no friends or allies, and give them nowhere to run. Make it so their own country wants to hunt them down and give out a reward for doing so. You have to make it so that their own spouse cannot trust the words they speak. If you take away everything that makes them feel safe, they will be so scared that they will be afraid to sleep. You will then make them feel like death is their only friend, but they will not take their own life for fear of their family's fate. NOW that is HOW you MESS with someone and that is exactly what Daniel and I were going to do to Pavel and his crew.

Finding Amelia was the number one priority. The reason being is that she is an analyst for MI5 in charge of her own team of agents who decipher classified intelligence. If her enemies knew any of the information she knew, it would be disastrous for the UK and its allies. Daniel met her while on the job in Eastern Germany and after they got married, she transferred from MI6 to MI5 to take care of their twin daughters.

We met with Keith just outside the club. We went through ever moment of the night, from the moment we arrived until the shooting took place. Keith wanted us to go back into our subconscious to see if anything was out of place that we might have initially overlooked. Looking at Keith, all I could see was Marlon Brando as Don Vito Corleone in The Godfather.

Between Daniel and me, nothing out of the ordinary came to mind. It was not until a few minutes later when I saw a taxi drop off a couple, who headed into a Scottish pub, that I realized how they knew where we were last night. I remembered seeing the taxi driver, who dropped my wife and me off, at our hotel on the front desk phone, moments after we arrived. I also remembered that his English accent was not of the Scottish locals but that it had a hint of Eastern Europe, even though he tried to hide it. You would think since he was working in the UK he would have learned to disguise his voice to sound more like the locals, but he failed because I caught it.

We sat down with a sketch artist and after I describe the drivers face, we had a name. My taxi driver was Dingus McFaddin. Dingus is a hired hand from Russia whose job is to provide the KGB with information on inside happenings in the UK. His job is simple. It is to spy on the locals as a taxi driver and report on diplomats and political figures. He is a typical spy planted to look like one of the locals. The only untypical thing about this spy was the fact that his handler is The Madam, Anna Layata.

I do not know if you feel it, but right now, I was feeling set up. Like someone sold out my location to the Russians. With the amount of taxi drivers in Edinburgh, the odds were that I would get a random driver who had never seen my face. Instead, I got the one drover in the entire city that not only knew who I was but worked for the one woman trying to put me out of my misery and then put me six feet under. Either I am the most unlucky person in all Scotland or someone close to me set me up.

If someone set me up and it feels like someone did, then it had to be someone within the CIA or my wife's Georgetown University department. Since no one in my wife's department had any problems with her and all her colleagues liked her, I ruled out her job. That leaves six people within the CIA that knew exactly where I was going on vacation. I was not sure which one it could be and did not want to speculate until I had more evidence.

As my wife recovered, Daniel and I tracked down

cab driver Dingus. After a day and a half, we got his cab to come to my hotel to pick up a major player in the illegal arms business. That is what we made Dingus think. With MI5's help, we spread the word that a major arms dealer was going to be in the country and that he was going to need a personal taxi service. Our information was only half-true because former IRA gunrunner Sam Schultz was in Edinburgh. He went rouge and started selling weapons to the highest bidder, while even selling out other members of the IRA in the process. He needed a taxi service out of the country.

What we failed to mention on the wire that Dingus was sent was the fact that Sam had been held at the US embassy for the past week waiting to be sent to London and then to be tried in an international court for selling weapons to the Uganda National Liberation Army from 1982-84. This information was mostly a secret, such that even most media outlets did not know about it.

Our plan went just as we had hoped, with Dingus picking up Daniel thinking he was Sam and that he could get his hands on a significant number of arms for The Madam and Russia. Even you would have gone through with this plan seeing the limited options that we had in front of us. Daniel had Dingus drive him around town for a while, all the while acting all paranoid. We wanted "Sam" to have the appearance that he was trying to escape from someone or something. Daniel promised Dingus a significant reward, which just happened to be a huge number of weapons, if he could help him get out of the city and then the country.

Being an opportunist, or so he thought, Dingus drove his cab south out of the downtown city area. They got on Comiston Road and headed toward the Edinburg Bypass on their way to Glasgow were Dingus had contacts that could smuggle anything out of the country. MI5 caught them at a planned point just a few blocks south of the Fairmilehead parish church. Daniel put a gun to the back of Dingus' head and forced him to stop the car where MI5 approached and apprehended him. Some of you may have drove faster or tried to injure Daniel if you were Dingus, but he did the right thing because he values life more than death.

Dingus, with his cold black eyes and his four-inch bar brawl scar, looks like he is the toughest guy you could meet. At five and a half feet and built like a Hell's Angel biker, he looks like he could hold his own in a fight. In reality, this is not the case. We put Dingus in a dark room and strapped him to a chair. After an hour we came in the room with a bunch of auto mechanic tools and put them on the table in front of Dingus.

I took the monkey wrench and started to tighten it over Dingus' hand, while Daniel started to ask him questions about his operation and connection with Pavel Korinniko. I got the wrench just tight enough that his hand could feel the two parts of the tool tightening around his bones. About this point in our interrogation, Dingus started spilling everything he knew about Pavel and all his friends. He told us that we should head to East Berlin and look for an I.D. counterfeiter named Wilhelm Shlekneil whom Pavel uses often and trusts like a brother.

Dingus told us about a Middle-Eastern man named Mohad el Zelconti. Mohad is Pavel's Afghanistan contact where he moves weapons to all Russia's Middle-Eastern allies. We learned that Pavel has a wife and three children, a boy and two girls, who live just east of Moscow in a town called Lyubertsy.

Our plan was simple on paper. We were going to Copenhagen, Denmark and from there take a boat into Germany and sneak our way into East Berlin. Yes, we had our Russian identities, but that did not guarantee Daniel and I was going to make it into Germany without authorities catching us. The good news was that Findrak Fiendra made our identities, and to this point, they were just as good if not better than a cover I.D. from our own agencies.

Flying into Copenhagen, Daniel and I took a day to gather ourselves before the first phase of our mission. It had been three weeks since the incident in Edinburgh, and there was still no sign of Amelia. Daniel could only hope and pray that she was still alive. We took a boat across the Baltic Sea to Stralsund, Germany.

We took a train from Stralsund to the East Berlin district of Pankow. From there, Daniel and I made our way to the Palasthotel located in the Mitte district on Karl-Liebknecht-Straße, one of East Berlin's major streets. This is a hotel for guests of East Berlin and the German Democratic Party. It is not a place for the locals to stay. I was a little scared to try to get a room.

The Palasthotel has several hundred rooms with many of them adorned with video cameras and they are teeming with listening devices used to monitor guests of an interesting nature. With all eyes and ears on Daniel and me, you can see why I am a little scared. You would be too if you were in my position; I am sure of it.

From the moment Daniel and I got to East Berlin, we used our Russian identities. They consist of Daniel known as Nikolai Gudenchki (a Lieutenant Colonel in the

Soviet Army) and me known as Romani Gudenchki (a Major in the Soviet Army). Our cover story as we were using was that the KGB sent us as officers to assess security around the Berlin Wall and that it was a surprise inspection. We even had MI6 come up with phony papers to help with our story. Our cover story was not one I would have liked, but as you will learn after time in the field, you sometimes have to go with what you have or the information told to you while in the field. Rather you like it or not, that is sometimes the way it goes in the field.

We spent a seemingly quiet night in our hotel room. We assumed that the room we were given was bugged and being watched by the Stasi. For those of you who do not know whom the Stasi are, they are the East German Secret Police. Daniel and I took a drive down the Karl-Liebknecht-Straße to a place called St. Mary's Church. It is a church of the Lutheran Protestant faith. The first historical mention of the church was in the year 1292. The church, reconstructed after WWII, looked more like a modern German church, which is why it has a red brick like appearance.

The reason I wanted us to stop at this church was the fact that one of its preachers was a CIA implant into Eastern Germany from the Western Germany city of Bonn.

Our contact was a short man standing no taller than Michael J. Fox does. He looked as if he only ate two meals a day for the last few years. His eyes looked bigger than a quarter and he had a nose that would rival Jimmy Durante. He spoke with a thick German accent.

I went up to the table on the left side of the room and I lit a candle. Then I went and prayed in front of the huge cross near the front of the church for only a few moments before I blew out the candle that I had lit, turned it upside down, and etched a cross into the bottom of it with my fingernail. I followed it up with a donation to the general fund in the offering basket and left the church. After I did the CIA "ritual candle lighting," our contact followed me, as I walked out of the church. I then followed him into a confessional like small room where we could talk for only a moment or two.

At first, he thought I was his new handler. With some convincing, I told him that I was just an agent looking for information on a target. My contact knew nothing about a Stasi by the name of Wilhelm Shlekneil. Would you blame him? I would not for it is like asking for a specific cop in New York City. It is not as easy as you think. My partner is either in a church praying for his wife or going nuts waiting for me to return. Therefore, I had to come up with a new line of questions. You would do the same with a mission on the line such as this.

At that moment, I remembered Dingus saying something about a passport to anywhere. Seriously, who in their right mind names their child Dingus? Once my grandpa told me that a person should never give their baby a name that will get them beat up. I think it is good advice.

Instinctually, I quickly asked him about the man known as the Passport to Anywhere. Immediately, his eyes got twice the size as he perked up. His advice was for me to go home for the man I was asking about would kill me if I went looking for him. Wilhelm is a man with many connections and only by his choosing does one get his services. I reassured this priest that my mission was to put Wilhelm out of business. The last thing I learned from my contact was that I should make my way to the Palast der Republik.

The Palast der Republik would be an easy building to find. It is located on the banks of the Spree River in East Berlin's Marx-Engels-Platz. It would be easy to find do to it being the only building in the city that has bronze tinted windows. The only problem would be getting in the building that was sure to be crawling with security. The building houses the German Democratic Republic parliament.

Daniel and I spent the next few days watching security and government officials as we took notes in a small notebook. If it were up to me, I would just walk in, put a bullet in Wilhelm's kneecaps, and then hit the road. Daniel constantly had to remind me that what we were doing was going to keep our cover story intact so that we could make a clean getaway when the mission was over.

On the third day of gathering information for our fake inspection, Daniel noticed a robust man with a Makarov pistol and four bullets tattooed on his left arm as well as a visibly deformed right hand. He was leaving the Palast der Republik with a manila envelope and Wilhelm Shlekneil was standing in the lobby just beyond the front doors. Seeing the man just about scared Daniel right out of his boots.

Daniel told me all about the man we saw with the envelope. I learned that on Daniel's mission right before we met, he was in Greece trying to stop a sale of nuclear grade chemicals to a Middle Eastern tyrant. Viktor Planktica was the Russian selling the chemicals on neutral ground. Daniel put a halt on the sale by scaring the tyrant in to believing the Russians wanted to assassinate him instead of do business with them. In the end, he had a showdown with

Viktor, and put two bullets into his right hand and shattered two of his fingers. This was with the warning that if he stayed in business there would be a bullet with his name on it.

The thing that scared Daniel the most about seeing Viktor in Eastern Berlin is that Viktor is actually a member of the KGB and not a spy impersonating one. After much deliberation on the subject of Viktor, we decided that I would talk with Wilhelm and that Daniel would carry on our fake security mission. I figured that Viktor has never met me, so I could hang around the Palast der Republik as a KGB officer and talk my way out of any disbelief over my cover story. Talking out of a bad situation is one of my specialties.

I walked right into the Palast der Republik, and upon doing so, a very ugly woman stopped me. Think of the ugliest woman you have ever met having a child with the ugliest man you have ever met and this woman would be uglier than their child would. She asked me all the questions you would think a secretary would ask a stranger. I explained to her about the security mission I was on and that I needed to talk to a high-ranking Stasi. She was reluctant at first but after I gave her a few compliments and asked her out to dinner, she called for two government officials to come down and talk to me. The thought of dinner with her made me want to puke and as you know, I intended to break our dinner date.

Both of the men looked at me as if they had no idea what I was doing there. We stood in a huge lobby with ceiling lights every three feet. There was a couch and three chairs positioned in a half circle facing the elevator and there were two visible video cameras, with one facing the furniture and the other facing the entrance. Behind the front desk and to the right was a long hallway with several rooms on either side of the corridor.

The two men in front of me looked like typical bureaucrats with one taller than the other is. The taller one was a little fatter in the face and I could tell the shorter fellow had leg problems because he was leaning on his left side and using the counter to hold him up. I explained my fake security mission to the two gentlemen and they laughed it off telling me they heard nothing of the sort. They turned and started to walk away not wanting to bother with me. You and I would probably do the same if we were they.

At this time, I raised my voice and told them that I would involve their superiors and government officials if I did not get what I came for. The short man with his beady little eyes dared me to, acting as if my threats did not scare him. In moments like this, you have to think fast because one decision can cause your mission to live or die. When I told the secretary to get me General Hielmshmel on the phone because we are good friends, the two stopped in their tracks and practically begged me not to involve the General.

I knew of the General because he is on a CIA watch list, but I was completely lying when I said I knew him. It is not as if you would have had a better idea if you had the same information as I did. I had the men, who were now cooperating without trouble, set me up in a small room where I could meet with a few members of the Stasi to assess security protocols.

After I interviewed a few people, I asked for one last interview and that the men could go back to their work all the whiles forgetting this meeting ever happened. When the last soldier got down to the lobby, I made myself scarce. The soldier was very muscular in the arms but otherwise looked as if he enjoyed one too many baked goods. When he was about to make his way back upstairs I came into the view of the man looking very unkempt. I made my hair look messy and tore my shirt on the sleeve and at the bottom.

I gave the soldier the most made up piece of crap story I have ever thought of and in my position so would have you. What I told him was as follows:

I was a former associate and good friend Andrenie Korinniko. When he died, I began to work for his brother, Pavel, because of my particular set of skills. My only problem was that I have been gambling and that I will bet on anything. I got in trouble and loads of debt with the mob and since I cannot pay my debt, they want my head on a platter. I told this man that I needed to hide and to do that I needed a new identity. I told this man that Pavel recommended that I see him and that he would help me in my quandary. I even showed him the scar on my right shoulder to prove that they tried to kill me.

That story was pure fiction and the only true thing I said was that I have a scar on my right shoulder. I got it in Cambodia in 1975 when I was shot and left for dead by Anna Layata. The man demanded that I pay him half the money up front and the rest on the day of the pickup. He mentioned that the only reason he took my job was due to my association with Pavel and my knowledge of his operations. Lucky for me that I remembered a few bits of information about Pavel during our briefing by MI5.

I left a bag of German currency in the janitor's

closet under a bucket, just as Wilhelm had asked me to. I got the bag from Daniel who got it from a MI6 safe house within the city, which has supplies and some cash for agents on the run. Wilhelm took a picture of me in his office and told me to come back in two days to pick up my passport and identity as well as bring the rest of the cash that I had owed him for the job. He told me that the passport would be full proof, and that I would be able to travel anywhere in the world that I wanted and the mob would be none the wiser. Not sure if you caught it, but there seems to be a lot of mob involvement or mention on cases I have worked.

Along with Daniel, I spent most of the next two days talking to people about a subject of which I could care less. The only good to come out of these two days was the fact that I could send the CIA a big detailed package of information about the inner workings of East Berlin's security, including some of its major players. To this day, and I think you can see why, I still do not understand why so many Germans were zealous to share security information with two complete strangers just because we spoke perfect German and Russian.

Wilhelm told me to meet him in front of the famous Fernsehtrum (television tower is how it translates in

English). It stands just less than 1200 feet high and about two thirds of the way up there is what looks like a big but minis Epcot Center building from Disney. There is no structure taller in this country and tons of people walk passed it daily. It is located in the Mitte district and from St. Mary's Church it is visible in the background. It is located in the downtown area and therefore there are many high-rise structures nearby.

There are a few apartment complexes in the area. Most of the buildings have that 1950's and 60's post WWII style architecture. Wilhelm blindfolded and put me in the back of a German BMW sedan as we drove down the Friedrichstraße road toward his apartment located on the banks of the Spree River in the southern part of Mitte.

With my blindfold taken off, I was in front of an apartment complex that stood about three stories high and probably had one hundred different apartments. Out in front there were several trees tall enough to shade the rode below. The road in front of the complex looked barely wide enough to drive two average size sedans down it. From the front of his apartment, we could see into the Mitte suburb. Out the back of his studio style loft, we could see the Spree River. A little ways down the riverbank and you will come across the bridge for the busiest walkway in the area.

His apartment was pristine and looked as if no one had lived in it for a few weeks. It was a studio style with the kitchen just off to the right of the entrance. As you walked into the apartment there is a sliding windowpane like door leading to a small balcony overlooking the banks of the Spree River three stories below. There was no television in this place but he had an exceedingly large brown couch with a glass coffee table next to it. Down the hall, from the back of the kitchen, was a bathroom. There was also, what I presumed to be his bedroom.

His beige carpet looked as if no one had walked on it ever. I could see a dresser full of shelves with small statues and trinkets but there were not any personal objects or photos. You are probably thinking the same as me; that in his line of work there is no time for a family. On his wall, there was a painting of a countryside farm, and it looked familiar. I think it might have been one of the paintings stolen by the Nazi during WWII, but I could not be sure. A small closet room down the hall is what Wilhelm had entered, and you might be thinking the same as me. I am almost certain that the room is where he does his work with making false documents and passports.

I do not get scared often but the look in Wilhelm's face somewhat crept me out. His brown eyes looked as if they were on fire, as he demanded I tell him who I really was. I told him that he was crazy to think of me as anything other than an officer of the KGB, but that fell on deaf ears. He kept rambling on about his informants and how they swear they saw me with a known MI6 agent.

VIKTOR, he must have seen Daniel and me in front of the Palast der Republik the other day. Then again, one point five percent of the population in East Germany is an informant for the Stasi. I sure hoped that Daniel was not far from where I was because this situation was getting worse by the minute and Wilhelm looked like a time bomb about to blow.

He came right out of the small kitchen and came right at me, pushing me against the wall with a steak knife aimed at my jugular. Once again, he asked the same questions and demanded answers that I swore I did not have. He put his right arm against my chest as he pulled the knife back with his left. Right before he tried to stab me, he took a half-second hesitation allowing me to slam my knee into his groin. My left hand grabbed the back of his head as my right forearm pressed against his Adam's apple.

He dropped the knife as he started to pass out, but before doing so, he hit me hard enough in the stomach that I had to let go of my hold. We struggled while holding onto each other until he slammed my through the glass door and onto the balcony. You could hear the glass shattering from the streets below as I was hanging half over the balcony. I had just enough strength to hammer his temple with my right fist.

His grip was loosened just enough that his face was met with my right fist, two left hooks, and a right cross that sent him stumbling back a few steps. He regained his balance as he ran at me and tackled me right into the guardrail. For a moment, everything went black as the pain shot from my lower back straight up my spine.

When I opened my eyes a moment or two later, I saw a hammer hit Wilhelm in the kidney as he hit the ground screaming. Daniel could not have come busting in at a better time. Daniel had followed us to the apartment so we could ambush Wilhelm there. Racked with the pain from the kidney shot, Wilhelm's face showed it as we put him in his beige lazy boy style chair located in the corner by the broken glass door. I grabbed the knife off the floor as I told him not to do anything stupid.

We gave Wilhelm a moment to gather himself as we began to put in the picture our story to scare him into distrusting Pavel. We proceeded to give him our speech about our problem with him. We told a story about how we had one of our assets captured in Italy because of a mistake on his passport made by Mr. Shlekneil, which we obtained from our contact. We also told Wilhelm that we came to find Mr. Shlekneil to deliver a message about not screwing up again. Due to the screw up, we mentioned that we wanted to give Wilhelm a warning and a reminder that the next mistake would be his last. The last thing we told him was that his client whom we got our passports from sends his love.

For those of you who are wondering the actual truth is as follows. We, as you know, were in Germany to get Wilhelm to distrust Pavel. A team of British agents, working with the Italian government, caught a Turkish couple using a Greek looking false passport. Authorities detained them before they could bomb the British consulate. Pavel sent the couple on orders to stop a British diplomat from meeting with Italian officials.

Right before we left, I took the hammer and hit Wilhelm's stomach with the end of the handle. What we did next made me want to throw up. The image is one that will always be stuck in my brain. It was something we had to do to further our mission of putting Pavel out of commission. I held Wilhelm's left hand down as Daniel drove a three-inch nail into his index finger. Like Mr.

Miyagi in the Karate Kid, Daniel drove the nail all the way through the bone in one swing of the hammer.

Blood shot all over the chair and floor as Wilhelm let out the most blood-curdling scream of agony and pain. Pounding nails into a person's fingers is Pavel's signature interrogation technique and Pavel uses it to send a message of fear for those who have crossed him. It is something that Wilhelm would have known being friends with Pavel for so long. I will never forget the sound of his bone breaking as the nail drove into his index finger. I think that now you can see just how we were going to scare Pavel's friends and colleagues to distrust him. It was going to be by using his own technique and making them think that Pavel sent his "goons" to attack them; in turn making Pavel's friends think he may do it again.

As Wilhelm passed out from the pain, Daniel and I decided to leave Germany and head onto the next part of our mission's objective. We left Wilhelm's apartment and head for the elevator. Just as we turned the corner and could see the elevator, it opened and out came a tall dark haired man with muscles like a NFL linebacker and a brown-eyed stare like a lion on a feeding hunt. He came off the elevator with two buff and robust KGB officers and four Stasi police.

We overheard them talking about heading to Wilhelm's room and that the two suspects they were after had to be taken alive, dead if necessary, but cautiously for they were dangerous MI6 agents. They were obviously talking about Daniel, and they figured I was his MI6 partner. It did not matter that they had the agencies mixed up because they wanted us out of the picture and were willing to kill if they had to.

Having no weapons other than a hammer, we ran back toward Wilhelm's apartment with no plan. On coming up, Daniel had noticed a stairway at the other end of the hallway from the elevator. With Viktor right on our heels, we ran down the stairs like it was an Olympic racing event and we were fighting for first place.

When we got to the ground floor, we could see two Stasi covering the front entrance and there was on Stasi on either side of the building in case we came out the back entrance. Daniel could see the guard on the left side of the building had a photo of his face, so I became the distraction. I walked around the side of the complex and stumbled as if I had just finished a full bottle of bourbon.

The man asked me to get back in my apartment and that they were allowing no one to leave until a couple suspects were in custody. I stumbled into him, laying my right shoulder into his chest with enough force to make him take a step back. With his athletic build and rough looking exterior, I am surprised that I pushed him back with little effort. He pulled me off the ground and I thought for a moment that he might put a bullet into my lungs and carry on. Even you could see in his black eyes that he wanted to.

The very moment I noticed he had pushed me away from his body; I fell into him with a left and two right punches in his body builder stomach. I followed with a right forearm across his face, which put his lights out. I took his Luger pistol and an extra clip because I did not want to be seen carrying a large rifle in East German territory. Any one of you would have left the rifle behind for the same reason I did. Some of you would have grabbed the rifle just because it holds more ammunition, but it makes you a bigger target.

I ran to the other side of the building, put the pistol to the soldiers head, and told him to put all his weapons and ammunition on the ground as I instructed him to lie on his stomach. I the hit him with the butt of the Luger pistol across the back of his head, putting him out cold. I gave the second soldiers pistol to Daniel as we plotted our next move. Every KGB liaison in the East Berlin district of Mitte was looking for us, so it was going to be like running through hell just to get a couple of miles to the famous Checkpoint Charlie.

Checkpoint Charlie is a few miles south of us in the Friedrichstadt neighborhood. It is open to western allies and is the only checkpoint that the East Germans will allow passage with proper paperwork of course. It was going to be extremely hard to cross that checkpoint because, on the eastern side, there are several soldiers checking incoming vehicles and the giant watchtower makes sure no one gets across unauthorized.

Daniel and I decided to split up and meet at the consulate in the British District of Western Berlin. Daniel took out the guards in the front of the building, and instructed me to hot wire Wilhelm's car. He told me to take the car and make a run for Checkpoint Charlie. He ran to the edge of the riverbank and jumped onto a passing riverboat like he was a Hollywood stunt man.

This was about the time that Viktor and his crew realized that Daniel and I were not in Wilhelm's apartment and that we were trying to escape the area. As I turned the corner and headed toward the car, I heard a door open and someone shouting instructions in Russian. I grabbed the rifle off the knocked out soldier and unloaded its clip on the entrance door to the building.

As you can imagine, that only bought me a couple seconds of time. I got to the blue BMW and opened the door, leaving it open to provide me with a little cover. While I leaned in and started to wire the car to start, Viktor's men started to open fire in my direction. The windshield shattered in the crossfire and so did the window in the open door. Bullets riddled the door as well as the seats in the car.

The moment I got the car started, I had only two goals in mind. First, I had to get back to the Palasthotel to grab the Russian passports of Daniel and me, as well as our security notes gathered during our fake KGB assessment. Second, I had to make my way south to Checkpoint Charlie.

I drove through traffic as if I was Adam Wets' Batman chasing a criminal in the Bat mobile. I was bobbing and weaving in and out of traffic with Viktor and company not far behind me. I also had two Stasi police join in the chase. I took a couple street corners fast enough that my car lifted two wheels off the ground.

You all know that you enjoy a good car chase in the movies because it makes for great entertainment. I agree, and the Steve McQueen movie Bullet is the reason for why I agree. In reality, car chases suck horribly. They are full of stress and are no fun at all unless you are an adrenaline junky. Those of you who are not fearless should not engage in vehicle chases for you will not get away or catch the one you are chasing.

I headed back in the direction of St. Mary's Church. In the distance, I could hear a train whistle blowing and it gave me an idea that I do not recommend any of you do. I think you can see where my thoughts were going at this point. I found and drove parallel to the tracks for about two blocks before I made the sharp left turn over the tracks narrowly missing the train.

The driver of the lead car pursuing me thought he could be as lucky as I was by beating the train. He could not have been less wrong. Like a semi-truck hitting a parked motorcycle, the train rammed into the right front side of the car turning it into a fireball of mangled metal being pushed into the air and off the track. The train derailed and headed toward the street and smashed into a bus stop before completely stopping.

With all the commotion and people scrambling for cover, I was free to travel to the Palasthotel. Most of the cities available police arrived to contain the chaos at the site of the train's impact. A few units tried to catch up to me on my way to the Palasthotel. I got to the hotel with no police anywhere in sight.

On walking into the Palasthotel, the clerk at the front desk tried to get me to stop by telling me that I had a missed phone call. The lobby looked like I was in a Marriott hotel and there were several people making tons of noise. Now, both you and I know that the clerk was only trying to stall me until the Stasi could arrive in the lobby.

We both know that he was trying to feed me a load of crap because only Daniel knew that I was staying in the Palasthotel. No one else who knew me knew where in the city I was staying. I did not even tell my handler Aaron where in the city I would be, only that I would contact him with updates.

I hit the stocky clerk right in the face, busting his nose as he hit the ground. I then ran up the stairs to my room. I grabbed our passports and our notes as I realized the Stasi were closing off all exits on my floor. I tied the two sets of bed sheets together and draped them over the balcony whiles tying them to the balcony rail. For your information, I only wanted to drop one story to the room below mine.

I could only hope that the floor below had less security. If you think for even a moment that I am crazy for trying this and should not do it, than you had better think about my options before you make assumptions because I only had TWO. They were simple: climb out the window or become caught by the Stasi.

I made it to the balcony of the room below and as I did, the sheets ripped. There was nobody in the room, so I left out the front door all the while making my way to the stairs at the end of the long hallway. All the buildings power, the Stasi ordered it turned off, in an attempt to try to impede my sight as the sun started to set outside. While running down the stairs, I ran into two Stasi officers of whom I had to shoot just to get down to the lobby.

I entered the lobby and someone greeted me with a fist in my face. As my eyes watered, the soldier grabbed my shirt as he pulled back to hit me again. I grabbed his hand on my shirt, pushed my thumb into the pressure point on the hand, and pulled his arm into an arm bar as he let go of his grip. With his wrist bending back toward his elbow, I took a step back and while throwing all my weight into the step, I tossed the man into the wall breaking his nose.

At the same time, a crazy tall blond-haired man ran at me with a knife and tried to stab me as if it was an ice pick. I used his momentum to push his hand around and behind his back where I push my elbow against his and toward the ground with his hand I had pulled to the ceiling.

I did it fast enough you could hear his elbow crack like two football helmets colliding on a hard tackle.

While holding on to the broken arm, I swung him around as to create a barrier for the third soldier running at me. I kicked the man I was holding in the knee, and he dropped to the ground as I let go of my grip. A man who had the build of George Foreman with the look of Evil Knievel lunged at me; while trying to grab me in his grip. I sidestepped him, grabbed his out stretched arm, and flipped him over the hardwood front desk to my left. While stationed in South Korea during the Vietnam War, I learned a little Hopkido from a local master of the arts. That is how I know how to do what I did and even though I am a boxing kind of person, this fighting style has its uses.

The same front desk clerk that I punched in the face an hour or so ago, called reinforcements from one of the Stasi stations within the hotel. We can all see that I only had a few minutes until soldiers and their itchy fingers ready to shoot and ask later, swarmed the lobby. After the collateral that I have caused, can you blame them for not wanting to ask questions?

I picked up the Luger I dropped, grabbed my bag, and briskly walked out of the dim lit lobby. I saw a Stasi police vehicle down the block, so jumped inside finding the keys under the driver's seat. I think I may have said this once before, but how stupid does one have to be that they would leave a car's keys in the vehicle for someone to steal it?

Some of my enemies call me adfero affero exitium, which loosely translates from Latin to mean the bringer of destruction. Adfero affero means to bring and exitium means destruction or ruin. I got the name because my enemies know that wherever they find me, destruction and chaos follow. Just think back to what I did to the Chosen Ones terrorist organization.

One reason that I have become this sort of persona is because I learned very early on in my career; you CANNOT lie down and TAKE whatever your enemies throw at you. One who lets their enemies walk all over them and does nothing about it should dig a hole and jump in it, for someone will eventually by planning their funeral. If you allow your enemies to do what they will without any reaction, you are no better off than a dead man, and for doing so, you soon will be.

What you should do is fight back with fear that no one will forget. If you strike enough fear into your enemies, they will welcome death before they bother to mess with you again. Victory is not about whom you beat, but how you beat them. That is how the world remembers your action. Also, remember that if you can face death and win than nothing stands in your way.

Not wanting recognition as the man raining down hell on this part of the city, I slid down in the driver's seat. I was able to dive a few blocks before the Stasi new where I was or that I had been driving one of their cars. I drove straight for the Friedrichstadt neighborhood making my way toward Checkpoint Charlie. I drove around in circles for an hour or two just to throw the Stasi off my trail.

It was near midnight when I arrived with Checkpoint Charlie in my sights. My only problem was going to be getting passed a guard shack with a huge spotlight checking for unauthorized East Berlin citizens trying to jump the gates. When the guards saw my car coming up the road, sirens began to wail.

Checkpoint Charlie has a large white guardhouse with a sandbag wall in front of it. There are buildings on either side, each a couple stories high. There are barricades on both sides of the guardhouse with a long road covered all the way across with more barricades that can be raised. Heading into the US sector, there is a long tunnel that one must pass through to get out of the Soviet sector.

In front of me was a four-story building with two

guards fully armed and a huge searchlight pointed in my direction. All I could see of the checkpoint was the large gates blocking my path to the US sector. The area was a little too silent even for late night on a Friday. I could see no one for at least a half mile and all the buildings had their lights off. It was darker than one would expect in a midnight Las Vegas blackout.

At the guardhouse used to check all vehicles entering or leaving the checkpoint, there were at least two visible guards, armed to the nines. The lengthy guard at the gate came a quarter-mile out from the guardhouse to get me to slow down and stop for an inspection. Even you know that if I stayed for an extensive car search I was not getting across the checkpoint.

I got out of the car as the guard asked and grabbed my bag as I exited the car. The guard radioed to the tower about me and the tower. I could barely see his face and his soft voice did not carry enough for me to hear everything he said. I caught him asking twice about the car and the fact that someone stole it. It was a typical Volkswagen police car, and other than the stolen report on it, there was nothing suspicious about it.

After a minute of searching, he got out of the car and pointed his gun in my direction all the while asking me to drop my bag and lay on my stomach. I did as he asked while waiting for him to approach. He walked toward me and bent to grab my bag. I shot to my knees as I performed a wrestler's double leg takedown by grabbing behind his legs and pulling them toward me as I lifted him off the ground. The guard hit the ground hard while firing bullets in the air on his way down.

Hitting him in the groin with my elbow, I pulled out the Luger and pointed it at him. The guard tried to make a move with his rifle, so I shot him in the chest before he could shoot me. I am sure that none of you would have done different and you will not convince me otherwise. This caused the two guards on the rooftop to try to become snipers by shooting in my direction. I made it to the car and started to drive it toward the checkpoint gate.

The sound of guns firing and bullets hitting the steel of an automobile echoed for at least a mile or more. For a moment, it sounded like I was Snoopy in a gunfight with the Red Baron. I did a barrel roll out of the car as the engine caught fire and slammed into the four-story building. Grabbing my bag full of false passports, documents, and notes, I pick myself off the gravel road.

Entering the guardhouse, I pistol whipped the only guard I saw in the building. Grabbing the Italian made Spas

12 shotgun loaded with flechette ammo, I headed out to the street to greet the oncoming Stasi vehicles. The explosion of the car into the tower lit up the night sky the same as Medieval knights shooting flaming arrows into a castle. Firing shot after shot at the front oncoming vehicle, I unloaded the gun.

The car lit up as if it were a gas stove exploding. All the cars behind it came to a screeching halt. They got out and started to fire on my position. I turned and ran, hopping over the barricade while several US military police started firing back at the Stasi. On showing my CIA identification, the MP's let me into the sector with little question. I turned and ran as fast as I could just in case a Stasi car made a run through the checkpoint after me.

I ran through the tunnel and kept on going till I ran out of gas. I had to of run two miles in right around ten minutes to make up the ground that I covered. I collapsed and could not move for at least twenty minutes. When I got up, I went to a nearby pub and used the payphone to call Langley. I told them that the mission to eliminate a major counterfeiter from the game was a complete success and that I was safely in the US sector of West Berlin. Langley gave me the location of a safe house I was to stay at until I received extraction instructions.

I left Daniel a message at the British consulate in British West Berlin. It took a day in a half for Daniel to get back to me, in which I rested while catching news of our mission's collateral. After we met, we decided to each go home and spend a week with our families while filling out mission reports and taking mandatory psychiatric debriefings. We also decided that I would travel to Russia to handle Pavel's family while Daniel would travel to Kabul, Afghanistan to deal with Pavel's Middle Eastern weapons distributor, Mohad el Zelconti.

I spent the better part of the next week with department shrinks, my handler Aaron, other higher-ranking officials, and my wife Athena. I took an extra-long week as I planned out the details of my mission to Russia. After two very good weeks with Athena, I was on a plane to Greece and then it was on to the Third Rome.

The Third Rome

It took some juggling of my travels, but I made it into Russia. I entered Greece where I boarded a train bound for Kiev, Ukraine. From there I made several detours on my way to The Third Rome, Moscow under the name Gudenchki. My travels took a little over a week and a Russian General whom I had been working with for some time put me up. To ease your thoughts that I see you are thinking, let me explain. My cover identity as you should know is Romani Gudenchki, a Russian KGB officer and Major in the Russian army.

My cover is that I am a KGB agent working as a mole in the CIA. I feed them low-level intelligence on US interest and on agents. I know full well that the agents I tell the KGB about are agents designated for 'retirement' by the Agency. They are agents who have turned on their country or have gone rogue by helping their enemies or selling secret to the highest bidder. The Agency has put these agents on a list of names designated for termination and if the CIA does not have to spend time and resources to do the job, then all the better right?

Moscow refers to itself as The Third Rome. Rome was the head of the entire Catholic Church until 1054 when it split into the Roman Catholic Church located in Rome and the Orthodox Church located in Constantinople (currently Istanbul). When the Byzantine Empire fell to the Ottomans in 1453, Moscow called itself the inheritor of the Orthodox Church due to its similarities to Constantinople. By moving the Orthodox Church to Moscow to remove the Muslim Ottoman control, the new Bishop declared Moscow the seat of Orthodox Church power and thus the successor of Rome twice removed or The Third Rome.

I told higher-ranking KGB officers, on entering the Lubyanka (KGB headquarters), that I had credible information on the imminent danger of one of its members and that I had to get his family out of the city limits because a US Black Ops team, on route, was planning to execute them. I embellished the story with other bits of information that had the officers intrigued but not really believing me. I am not sure that you would do any better than I have.

The Lubyanka is a large building. It reminds me of what it would look like to take three New York apartment high-rises of four stories and put them into one large building. Inside there were very bland colored walls with rooms that are evenly spaced. The first floor houses a prison and the KGB uses the rest of the building.

After walking a minute or two down a long and narrow corridor on the second floor, one comes on a room that is wide and open with several desks and metal cabinets. Off to the right corner of the room can be seen a smaller room with a large conference table and walls lined with photos.

If you saw this area of the building, you might think you were in a large law firm. The head of the department has a room the size of a corporate boardroom. Off to the left is an elevator that takes operatives to a training facility that includes a firing range and the prison.

The officers I talked with took several minutes to gather files and reports. After they had read the reports filed by the agents handler (the one I was telling them about), the officers dismissed me and told me to wait for further instructions on my new mission since they seemed to think I had blown my cover by coming to KGB headquarters.

I waited at an empty desk in the open room as the officers decided what to do with me. When they all had left the room, I entered and took photos of the file using a small camera I had concealed in my coat pocket. The camera, made by the finest tech boys in the business, looks like a pack of Greek made cigarettes. By the way, I do not smoke for I cannot take the smell.

One officer, a stoic and an emaciated looking man, came back to the room. I ran out of the room and down the hall to another room used to develop microfilm. After an hour, I left the room with photocopies of the file that I needed. Now it was on to getting a car and finding the family of the agent I had come to mess with. When I left the room, the emaciated officer started yelling to have me stopped before I left the building. Seeing my only worthy option, I quickly left the building the same way that I came in. I am sure that even you would have done the same with the limited choices available.

Doing what most people, including you, would have done, I hotwired the first car that I came across that was not locked. I was lucky to find a map in the glove box, so it was off to Lyubertsy to find the family of Pavel Korinniko. You know when you get the feeling that something bad is going to happen, but you cannot figure out what or why? That is exactly how I felt while on this thirty minute drive though Russian traffic.

Moscow is a beautiful city with a bustling industrial economy, even though it has a crazy government philosophy. The old part of town that I drove through has remnants of mid to late 18th century architecture. Driving by Red Square, I could see St. Basil's Cathedral in the distance to my left. The Cathedral is a late 16th and early 17th century representation of Russian architecture.

It has a brick red color due to its stonemasonry. On top of each of its eight church pillars, sit eight onion shaped domes, each having their own unique pattern and color scheme. Shades of red and green seem to be the colors most used on the domes. The brickwork, tessellated mostly of green and blue colors, gives the cathedral an array of colors like a painter's palette.

I also passed by the Kremlin. The Kremlin houses many beautiful architectural towers and many churches adorned with golden domes. In addition, it is where the heads of the Soviet government meet, just like how the US has the House of Congress and The White House. Built on the banks of the Moskva River, a wall connecting many of the towers and protecting the Kremlin from invading armies and outsiders encloses it.

I left the city of Moscow and took another fifteen-minute drive to the town of Lyubertsy. I had only one problem, and you would too in my shoes. It was just after Thanksgiving and I had no place to stay if this mission took any length of time. The days were getting colder and shorter and I am all alone on this mission. On this kind of mission, I thought Aaron would have given me a contact or a safe house, but the sleazy guy has been dodging contact with me because he has more pressing asset problems in Colombia.

Last time I saw Aaron, he sent me on a plane to Greece, and told me good luck. The worst part was that I had no resources and my main connection was in the southern hemisphere. The Agency left me without someone whom I could contact if I got in trouble. If ever the CIA meant their statement about us fellow agents being on our own in the field, and that they will deny us as agents if captured, than this would be the time.

It is in these moments that you must remember that stupidity never wins. In moments like this when the brain realizes that it is all alone, fear begins to set in. Some advice that I can give you on how to combat this is the following: a calm mind is a happy mind, while a disturbed and fearful mind is a lost mind. Rest is a key factor in these moments for a rested mind is an alert mind, and as I have said before thinking clearly saves lives.

Snow started to fall as night began. The moon became visible as its light became blinding while bouncing off the snowy ground. Tree branches bent to the near point of breaking due to the weight of the falling precipitation.

Houses, built in classic Russian architecture, billowed smoke from fireplaces heating rooms as snow covered sagging rooftops and lined window panes.

Some driveways had cars buried in the powdery wet snowflakes as garages and gutters had icicles thick as kitchen knives dangling from them. As I stopped near my targets house, I could see a couple bundled to the nines in fur coats covering their bodies to their knees, also with hats and gloves on. I could see their breath in the cold brisk air as they walked back to their house from a neighbor.

I parked my car at the end of the street to plan my moves and the next thing I remember it was daylight with children playing in the snow. I must have fallen asleep. I got out of the car and walked to the house of Irina Korinniko, Pavel's wife. A little dark haired girl between the ages of eight and ten answered the door. I assumed the girl to be Pavel and Irina's daughter Karina.

The little girl asked me about why I was there and who I was. I told her I was a KGB agent named Gudenchki and that I needed to speak to her mother about her father. I thought the girl was going to bring back a less than average height and slightly thick blondish gymnastics coach whom she called mother.

I should have expected, as you know me, anything

but that. Instead of a stout woman who looks like she ice skates with ten-pound ankle weights, I got a slim woman with a body type like Chris Evert and a face that looks like she could be Brooke Shields body double. The woman at the door inquired about whom I was and what I was doing at the house. I thought about playing it cool like I was a ladies man, but if any woman not my wife knew I was full of rubbish, I was staring right at her.

I thought I was going to install fear into the family. That I was going to come back in an hour or two and shoot up the house to give that created fears some realism followed by a kidnapping of Karina Korinniko. That was all before I met the woman who knew more about Pavel and his whereabouts than just about anyone on the planet did.

The woman invited me into the house and she led me into the kitchen. The house was not as big as I had pictured. It had a few paintings strewn on the lavender painted walls. There was a Russian children's program on the small television with a young boy watching oblivious to anything else. In a mostly empty room with wooden floors and a window allowing natural sunlight to illuminate the room, Karina was practicing what looked like ballet steps while leaning against a chair.

I took a seat at a small round wooden table in the kitchen as the red headed woman went to get her blond sister-in-law. It is bad enough that the last person I ever wanted to see answered the door, but NO ONE told me that her sister was Irina Korinniko. Some of you would have done the smart thing and bolted for the front door likes a gazelle running from a lion in the savannas of Africa, but I stupidly did not.

During the moments when the redhead went to get her sister, I thought she was going to come back with a shotgun and decorate the walls with my body parts as my blood stained the hardwood floor. Instead, I was served tea as both of them listened to the same story that I told to the agents back at the Lubyanka. After I was done telling them about Pavel and the danger his family was in, they escorted me out of the house and told me they would pack up and head out of town for a few days till thing blew over.

Even you could see right through their lies as I left their house. Moments later the redhead stopped me to ask me one more question. She wanted to ask me about how in the hell I thought I was going to get away with whatever I had planned. While I took a moment to think of my answer, she raised a shotgun in my direction and fired a beanbag round into my chest. It knocked me flat out on the snowy ground.

I do not remember much of anything after the shot until I woke up in a damp dark room with this very annoying sound of water dripping into an empty metal bucket. They tied me to a metal chair with a pool of water at my feet. I was also barefoot with clothes on that were wetter than a Navy Seals wetsuit after swimming to land. I could hear metal doors opening and clanking in the background along with the familiar sound of chains moving.

In all my years of chasing Anna Layata, I never learned anything about her family, and as far as I knew, she was not married. Not one bit of evidence in her CIA file suggested that she had a sister let alone be married to Anna's number two, Pavel. After being in the dark for what seemed like ages, Anna came in and began to ask me questions ranging from whom I really was to my mission and why I was in Soviet Russia. Other than calling myself Romani Gudenchki, I said nothing at all.

Multiple times interrogators whipped me until bleeding, shocked me till I passed out, and drenched me in water until my body began to shake. After a while, they threw a British agent in my room and we became friendly. Bernard was his name and the KGB charged him with stealing Russian military secrets. For as long as I was in this dark hole, I started to lose track of time. You would too if you were there as long as I was there.

Guards only fed us twice a day and we received a bowl of rice, two pieces of bread, a glass of water, and sometimes a slightly undercooked chicken wing. One time after I finished eating what tasted like day old food, Anna took me into a larger room and they tied me to a table. Anna then put a pair of headphone over my ears and began to play the sounds of car horns honking. The sound was so loud that my head hurt and brain started to go berserk.

Anna left the room and I was all alone with the loud sounds of horns blaring in my head. I guess she figured that if she could not make me talk she would make me certifiably crazy. It was about a few hours after she left that I heard the door slam open. A soldier with an assault rifle approached and cut the ropes around my wrists and feet. He then helped me off the table and out of the room. He shot two guards as we left the prison that was my home as of late.

We finally arrived at a safe house after a highly intense vehicle chase by four different KGB driven cars trying to shoot us as we drove away. A field medic attended to my wounds as Bernard slept on a couch. Never in my life have I ever been happier to see someone than I was in that moment, when Daniel Macradin walked in announcing that the coast was clear.

Daniel and I had a long conversation about what happened to me. He informed me that I had been in the Lubyanka prison for just over nine months and that he inquired about our joint MI6-CIA mission and me. He told me that the CIA had declared me missing in action and presumed I was dead. The CIA told Daniel that they had no idea of my whereabouts and that nobody in the Agency knew what I was working on or where it would have taken me.

If it was not for MI6 sending a team to extract Bernard, I would most likely still be in a KGB prison hole. I think you can understand why I was beginning to become increasingly angry. I KNOW FULL WELL that Aaron, my handler, KNEW WHERE I HAD GONE. He was in Greece when I got on the train to Soviet Russia and he was the one that gave me the gun and camera that I had on me when I arrived at the Lubyanka. He knew I was working with MI6 in trying to eliminate Pavel Korinniko and his contacts.

I was not going to forget what Aaron had done by lying when he said he had no idea where I was. I know he had something to do with my living in a cell for nine months. I know this because if the Director of Clandestine Services, Lester Penada, had any clue of my torture and stay in a Russian prison, he would have sent his own team to get me home.

I also learned that an American covert air strike hit a compound and killed six terrorists including Mohad el Zelconti. I also learned that Wilhelm Shlekneil had put a bounty on Pavel's head for what he thought Pavel had ordered done to him. I spent the next six months recuperating at home with Athena and our seven-month-old daughter Sandra. During my time at home, I learned that Pavel's body surfaced in the Black Forest Mountains in Western Germany on the banks of the Danube River with two bullets, execution style, in the back of the head.

During my time at home, I started plotting a plan to catch the mole within the CIA that was screwing with my missions. I had my suspects, with Aaron Greetox my handler being one of them. When I am done with my investigation, whoever was responsible for committing treason, by compromising CIA missions and American agents, will wish that their god they prayed to would have mercy on them. When I am done, The Devil would be scared at what I might do when I catch them!

The Pearl of the Danube

Peace as defined in the Webster's dictionary is an agreement or treaty to end a conflict or the threat of a conflict. This is what the world strives to achieve. People devote their whole lives and or careers in pursuit of peace. Two world wars ensued over this concept, yet the achievement of world peace is still unattained.

In the latter half of 1987, members of the Pentagon had summoned me. I had no idea what they summoned me for or what they may have assumed I had done. In my position, you would have felt the same and the summons might have perplexed you. The somewhat newly appointed ambassador to the Soviet Union, Jacob Malley, wanted to meet with me about heading a four man protection detail as he met with the Soviet Union ambassador in Europe about peace. The Pearl of the Danube Budapest, Hungary was to be the location of the meeting place.

The other three members of the protection detail were unhappy with me as the one chosen to lead the team. They all belonged to the Secret Service and you can understand their dislike of me leading the team. Two of them wanted an all Secret Service team and thought that I had no business on this trip because I was with the CIA.

The other member, having five plus years with the Secret Service, hated the fact that she was on the protection detail and not running the team.

There was on major reason that ambassador Malley wanted me to lead the team. He told me it was because the other three members of this team were knowledgeable in protecting individuals and that alone. He wanted me to lead because he knew that I had extensive knowledge of all the players that may or may not attend the meeting and the subsequent ball at the Hungarian President's mansion. He wanted someone who could not only identify threats but also identify key players who the other three might overlook if they do not seem as possible threats.

Jacob Malley is a burly dark-haired middle-aged man with a stoic personality. He was a senator during the Carter and first Regan administration before heading to the private sector trying to broker peace and put an end to the Cold War. In early 1987, he became the ambassador to the Soviet Union due to his dealings with Soviet companies and political figures.

Philip Axerdawn, one of the protection team members, is a three-year Secret Service member who has two black belts and an uncontrollable appetite for red heads. He is a typical blond-haired blue-eyed California

surfer looking man. He went to a high school in Santa
Barbra, California and yes, he was a high school champion
surfer.

Justin Mastord, a former military police officer, is
the second of three team members I have on this protection
detail. He has a body just like Sylvester Stallone's Rambo.
He has a know-it-all attitude and even though he takes
orders well, he complains about them if they make him
disgruntled. He has a big scar under his left cheek from an
altercation with a drunken soldier and he is easily
provoked. Justin still has his military haircut.

Jaena Meclau-Berkaw is a Secret Service agent
hailing from the Louisiana Bayou. She was a New Orleans
SWAT officer before joining the Secret Service, where she
has been for the last six years. Her black eyes can
sometimes seem cold, especially when she wants
something done. If not for my knowledge of the players
attending this conference, Jaena would have been the team
leader. For some reason Jaena reminds me of Sigourney
Weaver in the movie Alien. She has very good leadership
qualities and stands almost as tall as I stand.

We arrived in Budapest on a Tuesday, just after
lunch. We had until Friday for the ambassadors meeting. I
took the team to the Hungarian Parliament Building where

the meeting was going to be taking place. We spent several hours looking for possible points of entry and for places where potential assassins might try to hide.

The meeting was going to take place on the Assembly hall of the House of Representatives. The walls have a golden look to them and a somewhat gothic style of architecture. The seats in the room, arranged in a half circle pattern, have a couple story balconies overlooking the room. There are a couple entrances on either side of the ground floor and one or two entrances to every level of the balconies. Honestly, I can agree with you in thinking that Budapest is a strange location for a meeting of this caliber. You would think it would be in Switzerland or a more neutral country.

Most of the day, Wednesday, we went over everything we had observed with Ambassador Malley. I sent Jaena and Justin to scout out the Hungarian President's residents where there was going to be a huge ball after dinner and the meeting on Friday. Philip and I went over the plans we had for travel on the day of the event. Later in the day, I went over a list of all the people assumed or confirmed to be at the meeting. I even came up with a list of possible people that would like nothing more than to put an end to a meeting such as this.

If there was one person that I hoped to see try to stop a meeting such as this, that person would be the one you know that I cannot wait to get my hands on. I would love nothing more than to disrupt and possibly ruin a meeting such as this if it meant the end of Madam Layata. If you tempt fate, look for death. If you tempt death, call it fate. Anna Layata has been living in a fool's paradise thinking she has been tempting death and surviving by fate when the truth is that she has been tempting fate and I was going to bring her death.

Most of the day, Thursday, was spent meeting with UN officials about the importance of this meeting and why it had to succeed. Even you can see that my team did not need an official to tell us what this meeting meant to the possibilities of world peace. They made us sit in a small room at the US consulate as they told us how the meeting was going to go, and who was going to be attending.

The list that Ambassador Malley, Jaena, and I came up with was twice as long as the one given to us by the UN. My list of potential party crashers was the same length if not longer than the UN list of attendees. The meeting was so boring for they were not telling us anything that we did not already know. Jaena and I were so bored we played hangman on a sheet of paper we kept passing to each other.

It is times like this that even you would want to "shoot" someone and move on with your day. The meeting with the UN delegate was more boring than the most boring high school lecture you ever had.

Our team spent the rest of the day going over every possible route to the Hungarian Parliament Building and every possible way someone could try to impede us from getting to the building. We went over it, no thanks to Jaena and Justin, so many times it felt like my brain was going to explode.

Friday morning came and it was time to get ready for our meeting at two. Jaena and Philip got in black SUV with Ambassador Malley while Justin and I got into a separate SUV and drove around the riverbanks acting as a diversion. While along the way, my vehicle blew a tire and as Justin got out trying to change the tire, a sniper almost shot him in the head. I could not see where the sniper was located but I began to fire in the bullets general direction. After a few minutes, the bullets stopped and the area became quiet except for the distant thunder and the sounds of rain.

Until the end of the meeting, there were no more shootings or attempts on any one's life. I do not know how you would feel but something does not feel right, like this whole day is going to explode in front of our faces. After the meeting, Jacob went with some delegates to grab dinner before the big ball later in the day. Since the shooting in the morning, there was nothing out of place and it was making me highly uncomfortable. If you were anything like me, and some of you are, than you would also have been on edge almost expecting something to go wrong.

The Hungarian Prime Minister's compound consisted of a huge late 19th century style mansion and a guesthouse that serves as a place to entertain guests and foreign diplomats. The house has a kitchen with a personal chef and wait staff. It has four bedrooms and two master bedrooms as well as five bathrooms, three den rooms with huge fireplaces, a trophy room, and two places to eat dinner at tables able to hold fourteen dinner guests.

The guesthouse is larger than my own home with three bedrooms, a large family room, a kitchen, and several other rooms. Next to the guesthouse was another building that has a ballroom you would expect to see in a Victorian castle. The dance floor had to be the size of my homes entire first floor. It had seven or eight Victorian style chandeliers that each looked bigger than an average sized Italian moped. The dance floor had a rustic wooden look that was probably because of the years of use rather than made by a carpenter's hand.

Just off the dance floor was a row of ten tables on either side of the room. From the entrance of the ballroom, located on the opposite side of the hall and to the right, is a room that several bakers and other caterers use continuously to supply guests with traditional Hungarian desserts and different tasting wines and champagnes. Next to that room is a golden adorned and spiral staircase leading to a second floor consisting of several rooms used for changing clothes and storing dishware.

The ballroom has a bright golden yellow look with dark mahogany walls covered with paintings of castles and former members of royalty and leadership. As we entered the ballroom, the place, already packed, had diplomats from several European countries including Hungarian parliament members, Russian dignitaries, and our small American delegation. People were talking about how well the conference went earlier in the day. They were also talking about nuclear armaments and ways to make the threat of their use a distant memory.

Several of the attendees were members of the Western European Union wondering how this may lead to changes across the continent. People were dancing to the Forties style big band and swing music that was playing by the large band located near the stairs to the second floor. The band looked like a full sized big band orchestra and they played all the classics from Benny Goodman to Duke Ellington to Glen Miller and even some of Europe's famous composers. The Waltz and its variations seemed to be the dance of choice for most of those on the dance floor.

As Ambassador Malley started talking to familiar faces from the WEU, Justin, in his tuxedo, went to the farthest table from the entrance just near the stairs and sat down next to the band whiles looking into the service room. He was observing the wait staff and their movements, looking for suspicious activities or people who might pose a threat to Jacob. Philip, while trying to do his job, went on the prowl for the best-looking redhead he could find. I guess he cannot help himself, even while on the job. With his behavior, even you might see Philip as mostly useless to the Ambassadors safety.

I started to mingle with some of the guests as I drank a glass of champagne. I would have preferred to be drinking a Mai Tai but at an upscale event like this, beggars cannot be choosers. I figured I could best do my job by talking to people instead of seeming cold and distant while making myself seem obvious. You would do the same. Jaena was putting her blond hair into a ponytail as she was flirting with a rugged and not so attractive English fellow who kept going on about international investments.

After a conversation with the international banker, Jaena grabbed my hand and asked me to dance with her. She told me that the Englishman was boring and would not allow her to speak a word for he kept rambling on. She also wanted to dance, and she enjoyed a good swing dance. I figured being on the dance floor would give me many opportunities to check out the dancers and observe their behavior. You would do the same if you were I. You might even think it less conspicuous than standing around staring at random people.

Right as Jaena and I started to walk off the dance floor, a good-looking man with short dark hair and fair skin in a corduroy suit came and asked Jaena to join him for the Viennese Waltz. I went to ask Ambassador Malley's wife, Clarissa, if she wanted to dance while her husband was engaged in conversation. I would have preferred to be dancing with Athena, but in this moment, Clarissa was one of the best choices.

Clarissa's long cherry blond hair lays against her red glitter filled cocktail dress. Her high cheekbones accentuated her facial features. Both Clarissa and Jaena wore a black bolero jacket, which somehow looked better on Mrs. Malley than Jaena and her white blouse and black skirt. After the first dance, Jacob asked to cut in for a waltz with his wife. If you were I, you would think that everything was going smooth. That is until I met my next dance partner.

I started to make my way off the dance floor and headed to talk to Tony Brekweal, the British Ambassador to Russia. I never made it off the dance floor when a beautiful woman with light auburn hair and an athletic body with a soft skin tone grabbed me by the hands and asked for a dance or two. As I looked into her hazel eyes, I tried to grab my gun out of my shoulder holster. It is a Beretta M9, the current standard US Armed Forces sidearm, and it has become my sidearm of choice for the last few years.

I started to reach my right hand to my left shoulder where I holstered my gun and at that moment, the woman grabbed both my hands as she preceded to lead me in the Cha Cha. I wonder how you would feel at this moment, as I felt torn on what to do. Part of me wanted to put a bullet into Anna Layata as we danced and the other part of me wanted to wait in anxiety of what might come now that the Madam had arrived.

As you may recall, I have called Madam Layata a

beautiful and charming woman. Most of you see her that way and it causes you to have cloudy judgment on the actions that she has taken. Tonight, she had her slightly longer than shoulder length wavy hair draped half over her chest and the other half over her back. She had on a powder blue dress shirt that was unbuttoned enough to show her bosom and buttoned enough to seem either classy or promiscuous depending on how you look at her.

The three of us men in the ambassador's protection detail all looked like James Bond in the Dr. No film, tuxedo and all, except I did not have a bow tie. The suit I rented gave me a puffy like pirate shit instead of a tie. If the tuxedo I actually own was not being dry cleaned, then I would have worn it instead.

Even you would have figured that the other three members of my team gave no real thought to the threat posed by my dance partner. After a couple of dances, Justin came over to talk to me about one of the bus boys serving hors d'oeuvres. He was rambling on about how one particular bus boy was looking very suspicious. It was at that time that Anna slipped away and out of my eyesight. You have no idea how much I wanted to beat the crap out of Justin at that moment. This was the closest I had ever been to Anna Layata without taking a bullet or being beaten and I blew the chance to put her out of commission.

About an hour went by and the particular bus boy did nothing to raise suspicion that he would do anything. For your information, I was not letting Anna being in the building cloud my judgment of this wait staff member. He seemed a little off with his unkempt appearance and his clumsiness, but that just seemed like his natural demeanor rather than someone about to do something.

After watching some of the delegates dance for some time, I noticed an attractive dark blonde-haired woman who kept hanging around the ambassadors to both the Soviet Union and Czechoslovakian delegate. I gathered she was from one of those two countries and she had several of the men drooling over her. She looked to be almost six feet tall and wore this tight body hugging leather dress that came down only an inch or two past her waist. The dress was so tight that she looked as if she was going to pop out of the top of her dress.

The thing that struck me about her is that she had on an expensive watch that she kept looking at every once in a while like clockwork signaling that she was anxious for something to happen. When I went to introduce myself to her, she seemed distant while quiet and cold. This woman barley said anything to me, and I could tell she was not overtly shy because she was flirtatious and chatty with the ambassadors I saw her hanging around. She also kept looking around the room with her giant brown eyes almost as if she was anticipating something to happen.

The only person she spoke to that was not one of the two ambassadors I mentioned, was the ugliest waiter in the entire ballroom. He carried way more pounds than his frame should have to handle and half his face looked as if it had just been ran over by an overflowing garbage truck. With Anna lurking in the shadows, part of me thought this woman was working with the Madam and the other half of me thought her to be a bored call girl. I am not sure who you think she is, but if you are anything like me than those would be your choices of thought.

I know this dark-blond not to be some ones significant other because the Soviet ambassador's wife died just a year ago and the Czechoslovakian delegate introduced Jacob to his fiancée earlier in the night. It was also at this time that Jaena came to talk to me about Philip. Jaena came over to tell me that she had not seen Philip in over an hour and that Justin and she had not heard from him in that time either.

That is just what I did not need at this moment. Philip was probably off performing a full body cavity search on some promiscuous woman all the whiles getting his rocks off. What did I tell you earlier about Philip and his desires? I was right to think because of them that he would be useless. Even you could have guessed that and so could have a four year old.

I asked Justin to sneak his way upstairs and check for Philip. Then I asked Jaena to do the same in the kitchen whiles I filled in and stayed near Ambassador Malley. After a couple of minutes, Jaena came out of the kitchen with no sign of Philip and the staff had not seen him. After Jaena and I talked for a moment, she decided to get some air and take a walk around the perimeter to see if Philip had gone out for a moment.

I quietly went upstairs to see what was taking Justin so long to get back to me. I quickly checked every room and to my displeasure, I found Justin leaning over a dead body. What I saw made me feel uneasy and some of you might have had to leave the room. Lying on the ground was the body of Philip with a stiletto blade sticking out of his heart. Justin told me how when he found Philip's body his pants were at his ankles and how he pulled them back up. I had Justin stay with the body as I went to inform Ambassador Malley of what had happened.

I walked down the stairs and headed straight for

Jacob and Clarissa when something made me turn around. I turned around and at the bottom of the stairs standing right next to the band I saw Anna Layata staring at the dark blonde-haired woman whom I have mentioned looked suspicious. The dark blond woman hooked her right arm around the Soviet ambassador's left arm and proceeded to walk him out of the ballroom.

Anna looked like her hair was messy, her shirt had two more buttons undone while partially sticking out of her dress pants, all the while staring at the blond she was also checking to see if her makeup was out of place. From the look of things, it seemed like Anna had seduced Philip into thinking he was going to be getting some action with a beautiful red head, his favorite type of woman. It looked like she enticed Philip upstairs only to kill him with a stiletto knife.

Right then I decided to approach her through the crowd on the dance floor. I made it not half way to Anna when everyone could hear Justin yelling at a muscular man to stop or Justin said he would shoot him. The mystery man looked like a heavyweight boxer with distinguishing facial features like a slightly protruding chin and a jaw line that seemed as if someone smashed it into his upper cheeks toward his nose. The mystery man had on an unlaced tie and a freshly blood stained white shirt.

I swiftly turned around and motioned for Jaena to stop the blonde-haired woman from leaving with the Soviet Ambassador. Immediately, I turned back so as not to take my eyes off Anna for more than a few seconds. Just as a deer caught in headlights, I was not going to move my focus off Anna until I made my move to grab her. If you had been chasing Anna as long as I have, you would feel the same way I do and I am sure your eyes would not fixate on anything else. You can say whatever you want, but that is how I think you would really feel if you were I.

Out of the corner of my peripheral vision I caught a glimpse of the mystery man which made me and everyone else in the room turn our heads to see him jump over the second story balcony, do a complete aerial summersault like a gymnastic performer at the Olympics, and somewhat land on his feet. Justin ran after the mystery man and grabbed the balcony rail throwing his legs over the side as he jumped to the dance floor below. Justin fell right on a table that upon him landing, it lifted on to one side while plates and champagne flutes crashed and broke as they hit the ground.

After a moment of bouncing off the table like a child's bouncing rubber ball and rolling on the floor as if he were an object thrown for a dog to chase, Justin landed on his feet. He dusted himself off and continued his chase of the mystery man after picking up his gun.

When the mystery man got in my arms reach, I tucked my thumb under my index finger and with the ridge of my hand, I swung my arm, like a Ric Flair clothesline, hitting the man across the throat and collar bone. The momentum of his body, when it hit my arm, caused him to leave his feet and while spinning in the air, he landed with his face bouncing off the dance floor as if he was a chubby person bouncing off the water after a high dive cannon ball.

The blonde-haired woman had started engaging in a fistfight with Jaena and to make matters worse the blonde-haired woman brought a knife to the fight. The blonde-haired woman was swinging her knife as if she was carving up a hanging slab of beef in a butcher shop. If you remember, earlier I mentioned Justin talking to me about a suspicious bus boy. I caught the bus boy bumping into Justin only moments after I laid out the mystery man.

The bus boy then swung around and put his arms around Justin. One arm went around Justin's throat with a chokehold and the other arm came up and both of his hands clasped together to strengthen the arm grip and the hold. The bald, skinny, and tattooed freakish looking bus boy had such positioning on his hold that every time Justin tried to hit him and break the chokehold, the bus boy moved Justin or himself so he would not have to let go of his choke.

I made one of those rapid no time to think decisions that are all too common when in the field. You may have done the opposite of what I did and you may not agree with my choice. I decided in a moment's notice that I would leave Jaena to fend off the blonde woman and that I would aid in releasing the pressure on Justin's neck by taking out the troll-like looking bus boy.

During this time, I started to move toward Justin, I had drawn my Beretta in case I had a shot at the bus boy's head. Unfortunately, for Justin, the risk of shooting the bus boy and not hitting my teammate was too high for even me, one of the best shooters you will ever meet.

I charged at the bus boy as if I was a bull running the streets of Spain. Anyone looking at the situation, including you, would know that it was not looking well for Justin. The hold had caused him to lose enough conscious that he had dropped his gun and his body looked limp. Most of the people in the ballroom was both screaming and running for an exit or they were on the ground praying for their life. You would probably be doing the same if you were one of them.

Anna ran toward Justin with such ferocity as she dove to the ground. She started on the left side of the room and ran ending on my right side. She dove and slide across the dance floor feet first as if she was stealing second base in a baseball game. Anna grabbed Justin's gun as she came to a stop. She then turned over so that she was pointing the gun in my direction all the while telling me to drop my weapon and get on the ground.

In my situation, what would you do? You would have limited options, though. Would you try to shoot Anna before she could get a shot off on you, even though she already pointed a gun at you? Would you pick up a scared partygoer to try to shield yourself? Would you keep charging Anna and call her bluff? Lastly, would you drop your weapon and do as the Madam has asked?

I value my life and knowing there was no where I could run that would not get me killed, I dropped my gun and put my hands on my head as I hit my knees to the floor. If your opponent has you backed in a corner then you should go down swinging. Why run like a coward when you can go down like a hero. Now if you fear death, do not fight it for you will not win. One thing my grandfather taught me is that a wise man knows what he has at all times, while the foolish man knows what he has when it is too late.

I am not a foolish man and I had a plan. I was just not sure if it was going to work. I noticed that the bus boy had dropped Justin's body and I was not sure if he was dead. The busy boy then asked Anna what was the next part of the plan. About a minute went by while Anna was still talking about how the game was over and that I had lost. She kept telling me to pray to my god for I was going to meet him/her soon.

I love it when people start making assumptions without checking to see if the facts are true. I bet you feel the same. The whole time Anna had been talking to me, the bus boy had not moved and was waiting for his next assignment. I noticed something that most may have overlooked. One person lying on the ground proceeded to kick the bus boy in the groin hard enough to send him doubling over and to his knees.

At the same time, everyone in the ballroom heard the sound of a woman yelp. I turned around to see Jaena's white blouse covered in blood. One of the scared partygoers tried to open the front doors and just as they pried them open, the woman escaping bled out almost instantly when she took a shot in the stomach. From the echoing sound of the gun, I could tell the shooter had a high-powered rifle and that armed gunman and a few snipers covered the building exits.

When my head turned back to Anna, it was apparent that the bus boy had not made absolute that Justin was dead. With a sound similar to two football helmets colliding on the field, the bus boys neck snapped as Justin twisted his head like a beer bottle cap. I grabbed the three-inched heeled shoe that was within my arms reach. Someone must have run out of the shoe when the commotion started because there was no one near me wearing the same colored shoes.

Anna had turned to see what the noise behind her was and all she saw was her conspirator dropping to the ground dead. She fired a shot hitting her dead friend in the head. If you were I and you were holding a three-inch heeled shoe, what would you do? Some of you are thinking that you would never have picked up that shoe to begin with while the rest of you are pondering what to do with a shoe. Have you thought about it?

I threw the shoe over Anna's head making sure not to hit anyone cowering on the floor. The shoe ended up next to a short French fellow. One cannot ignore human curiosity and instinct. No amount of training shall get you completely to ignore those two qualities no matter how hard you try or train. With that in mind, Anna turned to look at the shoe and look where it landed.

Anna then pointed the gun at Justin, demanding that he not move and that he drop on his stomach. Not moving fast enough, Anna shot Justin in the right shoulder. She was very impatient and edgy, which made her actions seem atypical. Normally, Anna seems very composed and that nothing gets her agitated. Today, she was different from what I had seen in her before. Then again, she does like to inflict pain on her enemies.

Anna then pointed the gun at Justin, demanding that he not move and that he drop on his stomach. Not moving fast enough, Anna shot Justin in the right shoulder not being patient enough. She was very impatient and edgy, which made her actions seem atypical. Normally, Anna seems very composed and that nothing gets her agitated. Today, she was different than I had seen her before. Then again, she does like to inflict pain on her enemies.

This gave me enough time to hop from my knees onto my feet. While still being crouched with my knees bent and balancing on the balls of my feet, I lunged to my right. I did an evasive shoulder roll to my right and grabbed my gun all the while getting completely up on my feet. I fired a shot at Anna, purposely missing her. The intention was to scare the living crap out of her and to let her know that I now controlled the situation. You would have done the same and you know it. Especially, with the limited options available.

With my gun aimed at Anna's head, Justin walked over to one of the tables near the kitchen entrance. He grabbed a knife and dug the bullet out of his shoulder muscle. He then tore a huge piece of the tablecloth to make a rap to stop the bleeding. I can see some of you cringe as I describe Justin taking the bullet out of his shoulder. It takes a certain type of person to be like him and I can see some of you are not.

I approached Anna and she tried to fight her way out of her predicament. Not wanting to drag this out, I did what any of you in my shoes would have done. I slugged her across the face with the barrel of my pistol. While she was out cold, I used a few tablecloths to tie Anna to a chair as I prepared to gather information on her mission. I thought the threat of a bullet to the knee would be a good place to start.

I threw a glass of champagne in her face as she began to gain consciousness. When I yelled at her to tell me her plan, she laughed at me and told me to go to hell. That is when I cocked the pistol and proceeded to jam the barrel into her inner thigh, near her pelvic bone, whiles pulling her head back by her hair. The only noise she made was an involuntary reaction to the gun jamming into her and my hand grabbing her hair.

I gave her one more chance to answer my question and I showed her how serious I was about shooting her and not caring how she felt. I shoved the gun hard into her upper thigh as I deliberately jerked my hand at the last second so that my shot went through the wooden chair and not her flesh. I was going to enjoy doing everything to her that she had done to me in the Lubyanka prison.

Anna flinched in a reaction to the sound of the gun whereas Justin about tackled me. He told me about how cruel he thought what I was going to do would be. I had to reassure him that this was nothing compared to the nine months this woman put me through in Soviet Russia. Justin still tried to convince me that there had to be another way to get answers out of Anna. When dealing with someone like Anna, you will learn that nothing is off limits when it comes to gaining information because in your shoes she would do the same and not even blink.

I told Justin about how Anna was the type of person who would do the unthinkable just to get answers. I told him about how she once killed a four year old and a newlywed right in front of a man just to punish him for allowing a target to get away even though the target would have probably eluded her as well. I had to remind him that her innocent charm and drop dead gorgeous looks are her biggest assets and her enemy's biggest crutch and that underneath it all might just be the devil reincarnate.

That last statement of mine made Anna chuckle a little. I think it amused her and I think she found my last statement as more of a compliment than an insult. I was just telling the truth, and the truth does not lie.

After talking with Justin, I gave Anna another chance to answer my question. At this point, most of the people were picking themselves up off the ground and they all had eyes on me. I am not sure if that would have bothered you but I really did not care what they thought of my actions at that moment. Justin decided to listen to me and let me do my thing and that he would watch over the exits, which gunman still had locked from the outside.

I walked over the dead bus boy and dragged his body in front of where I seated Anna. It did not hit me until I saw his dead body up close, but the bus boy had been one of Anna's team members for over seven years. Remember when I told you about my mission in Amsterdam where I met Daniel Macradin. This dead busy boy was none other than Yuri Kuten, Andrenie Korinniko personal bodyguard from the club.

I ripped off Yuri's shirt, walked over to a table, and came back with a knife. Right in Anna's view, I was about to become a butcher and Yuri was going to be my slab of beef. She finally showed emotion when she yelled at me in a timorous tone not to desecrate Yuri's body. I put the tip of the knife on top of Yuri's arm and she about broke the windows when she screamed in terror practically begging me not to continue what I was about to do.

For roughly ten years, I had been trying to find Anna's kryptonite and it looked like I had finally found it. The one thing I learned about Anna was that she has no problem torturing others or seeing it happen to them as long as it was not someone with whom she had an intimate personal connection.

Some fears, no matter how hard you try, you just cannot hide. Some fears just overcome you and you cannot control them even to the point that they paralyze your body. As tough of a woman and spy as Anna is, here fear of seeing her close friends and family desecrated or killed makes her act the same as a claustrophobic locked in a unmoving non-operating elevator.

It was at this time that Jacob interrupted me,

wanting to know if I had a plan to get everyone out safe. Normally, I would have pulled Ambassador Malley out of the building because his safety was my mission priority. Even you can see that this situation was not normal and that two things kept me from my mission's priority.

The first was the Madam and stopping her plan. The second was the fact that I saw a woman try to leave and for trying, someone killed her. The thing that bothered me the most about the enemy's coup de grâce on the woman was the sound of the rifle that they used.

At this point, even you would have to figure that sniper fire or several armed guards covered the whole building. Based on this, I reckoned that the safest place was to remain calm on the dance floor as long as the men outside did not storm inside and stayed put. I am not sure about you, but I would rather be alive for the moment than take the chance at being dead for eternity.

I reassured Jacob that the situation was under control, that he should remain calm, and that everyone should go back to the way it was before all this began. I turned my attention back onto Anna, who looked like all the panic had escaped her mind.

The one thing you shall learn about this job is that if you let your enemy's control you while doing what they please, than you are as good as dead. Your family will be planning a funeral for you because that is all you will be worth to them, the price of a coffin. It is like a chess game in that your enemy takes one of your pieces, than you have to counter by taking twice as many of theirs.

You do not take what they dish out, but you fight back. You do not just fight back when your enemy attacks, you come at them continuously until they back down and run. It is just as I have said before. If you play to win than you look to lose, but if you come to dominate than you play for the win and do not forget it.

It was at this time that I decided to try something a little different. I grabbed Yuri's body and with Justin's help, we moved him over to the double door entrance to the dance hall. From the side of the door, Justin pushed open the door and ran back out of the line of sight of the shooter looking into the entrance. I covered myself and slowly walked out the door with Yuri's body as my shield. Soon as I was out of the doors range of motion, I dropped Yuri, grabbed the door, and ran back inside while closing the door behind me.

I ran from the left of the entrance and dove over a table, pushing it over to create a barrier of protection. I positioned myself so that I could see Anna and have a line of sight should I need to shoot at her. Justin, at this time, decided to run to the other end of the room and cover the kitchen exit whiles letting me handle the front doors.

Several minutes went by and nothing had happened. Right about now my adrenaline, and yours would be too, was pumping fiercely as I waited for those outside to make a move and show some of their cards. Most of the delegates decided to hide with most of them running upstairs.

I started setting up tables as if they were military barricades throughout the room. I took two of the bands microphone cables and moved them to the front door. I also broke a few champagne bottles and glasses into a tablecloth, which I carried to where I had placed the cables. I spread the broken pieces of glass out on the ground on front of the entrance.

I quickly stretched one cable across the bottom of the entrance door and tied it to a leg of a table on either side of the door that Justin had placed for me. The cable was about ankle height off the ground. Justin had filled two buckets full of water that he then dumped on the edge of the dance floor, near the middle of the room. As he did this, I cut off one end of the second cable to expose the wires under its protective sheath.

I plugged the cable into the music board and turned

it on. Sparks flew out the other end of the cable as the electricity flowed through it. This twenty-five foot cable would do just nicely for what we planned. It was at this time that Justin had cracked open one of the two front doors enough that he could fire a shot into the air toward the enemy outside.

While he was doing this, I was positioning Anna, still tied to the chair, so that her body was in direct sight of the entrance doors in case the sniper fired a shot into the room as soon as they opened them to clear a path for his comrades to storm into the dancehall. At this point I hopped the sniper would shoot Anna for I did not care if she lived or died as long as the ambassador, his wife, my team, and myself made it out alive.

Seconds after Justin fired his shot, he made it to the back of the room. I hide behind on of the barricades that I had quickly made near the middle of the room and positioned on the left side and closer to the wall than the open center of the room.

The doors opened from the outside and just as I predicted, the gunman stormed inside with their heads up, surveying the hall. Most people when they enter a room, they fail to check the ground level to see if anything is in the way. Angry people usually run in with tunnel vision, only seeing what is in front of them.

The first gunman to enter the room completely tripped over the cable as I had hoped and he landed face first into the broken glass. He had several pieces of glass sticking out of his skull and his entire face became covered in a waterfall of blood gushing out of the massive gash at the top of his head. One gunman ran in and headed to the right of the entrance. Crouching, he opened fire on one of the tables I had set up; all the while thinking that someone was hiding behind it.

After unloading his first clip, he reloaded his machine gun and all I saw was his gun firing into the air as he dropped to the ground dead. Jaena had pulled the knife out of the dead blond-haired woman and flung it into the gunman chest, killing him almost instantly. The whole time Justin and I had been readying for the enemy, Jaena had been regaining her energy and trying to stop the bleeding of her finger that she had cut in her fight.

Two of the men entered and headed straight for Anna. The team had now shown all its cards. They had come into the dancehall to get Anna out safely. As they advanced toward Anna, I bet you could guess what I was about to do. Now what would you do? I flung the cable into the pool of water on the ground and one poor fool began to convulse as he fell to the ground, electrocuted. The poor fool wore an expensive leather pair of boots that did not contain a rubber sole and for that, he paid.

I gave the other a bullet to the head. That makes three down and a few more to go. The rest of the gunmen, wanting to regroup, ran back out of the dancehall. It was this moment that I made a decision to get the hell out of this dancehall and make a run for it out the back of the compound. I had no idea how many assailants there were or how much firepower they were carrying. These questions are ones that anyone in my position would love to have the answers.

Moments after I talked over my plan with Justin and Jaena, they both went upstairs. They came down with Ambassador Malley, his wife Clarissa, and Ambassador Ilia Kovlenko who is the Soviet ambassador to the US. I untied Anna and put my gun to the back of her head, reminding her that if she tried to run or do anything I disliked, I would put a bullet in the back of her head. I also reminded her that I knew where her sister-in-law Irina lived and that the Grimm Reaper, disguised as me, would love to pay her a visit if Anna did not participate.

You may not agree with me, but for once, it was MY TURN to start using family as a bargaining chip. She had been doing it long enough. Do you remember when I was in the Athens of the North? She ordered that attack on my family and I would have left well enough alone but she brought family into this and for that, I was going to make her pay the price.

We ran out the back of the dancehall and exited through the kitchen. I sent Anna out first, just to test the waters. An idiot, who stands just below my shoulders with a crude haircut and beady little eyes, came up to Anna asking her if she was all right. He mentioned that the rest of the group was out front and that they were ready to cut their missions losses and retreat. I thanked him in Russian and being surprised he turned in my direction to see who was there.

I happily greeted him with the butt of my pistol in the center of his forehead, putting him out cold. I then mentioned for Anna to continue to move. We ran to the edge of the dancehall, with Anna leading and Justin carrying the rear of the group. If you are wondering why I was escorting the ambassador from the Soviet Union, it is because I am not sure if Anna and her team came to assassinate him or Jacob Malley. I played it safe by taking both with me.

Peaking around the corner of the building, I noticed

not a single person, so I had the group run toward a group of trees to our right no farther than twenty yards. Seeing that it was just past midnight and the air was cold enough to see ones breath, I figured the trees would provide coverage as we figured out how to make it to the gate at the back end of the compound.

We decided to make a run for the gate. On either side of the gate was a row of bushes that were about my waist high. Being quiet was out of the question because fallen leaves had littered the ground in this brisk autumn night. The nearest wall to the compound was at least fifty yards to our right and standing a story tall, the wall was unclimbable.

We made it not half way when a couple of assailants started to fire on our position. Justin fired back at them, telling the rest of us to continue through the gates. I shot the lock on the gate and pushed the large metal gate open. Fallowing the landscape to our right, you could hear the flowing waters of the Danube. In front of us were an open field and two football fields to our ten o'clock began what looked like and ever expanding woodland.

We followed the river for not a hundred feet before we could no longer hear gunfire. Instead, we heard footsteps coming toward us. A figure headed our way and it looked as if the figure was sprinting for a gold medal at the Olympics.

Justin was running in our direction and he was yelling at us to not only move but also do it quickly for a large group of armed men was not far behind him. Up ahead was a small dock with an above average sized boat. You could assume it belonged to the Hungarian Prime Minister. I thought exactly what you are thinking; that this was going to be our way out of this situation.

Right as we approached the boat, you could hear the sound of an engine getting closer as if it was approaching our position. The small dinghy pulled up to the other side of the boat and one passenger got onto the docked boat. At first, I could not make out whom the person was that hopped onto our escape vessel.

Soon as the clouds cleared, using the light from the almost full moon, I could make out that the body in the boat was a woman. No one, even you, could have seen what was coming next. No one, even you, could have prepared for the bombshell that was moments from hitting me.

The woman pointed a gun in our direction before any of us could draw our weapon for a standoff. This woman with a gun was another redhead but unlike Anna, her shade was more of a carrot orange red rather than auburn. She was tall for a woman and wearing a custom-made beige corduroy sleeveless ski vest jacket. Her sweater covered her arms in a dark bluish color. A quick look at Justin and I could see he was drooling a little over her fashion runway style figure.

Something about this woman was familiar and I just could not place it in this moment. There must have been a London style fog over my brain because I should have recognized her. She started to talk to me, and she even called me Joey all the while apologizing for what she had done and was going to do. Any one of you could have seen the hamster of my brain starting to turn the wheel without much speed.

Just then the moonlight peeked out of the clouds, and like a racecar spinning out of control after hitting the wall, it hit me exactly whom this woman was. I tried to get her to explain why she was doing all this, but clearly she was not the woman that I thought I knew. You could see my confusion because even my wife considered this woman a close friend.

This woman finally started talking and she told me enough to enrage me and slightly disappoint me. She told me of how her parents trained her since she was born and that they gave her no choice. She told me of how they raised her to be a Soviet spy and that she knew no other life. She also told me about her mission to infiltrate an enemy's government by gaining information from one of its agents.

She said she was set up to meet a British spy in Germany and that she was to get him to want to marry her. A traitorous teammate, she said, set up the British agent and she seduced him to the point that they ended up marrying. Her luck would have it that since she grew up in London from the age of two and the agent she married loved here so much, she got a job working for the British government.

She said she only had one regret and in her lamenting, she kept apologizing for the pain she had caused while hoping her husband would forgive her. Her only mistake in an otherwise working plan was that not only did she have children but she also committed one of the cardinal sins of spying.

Her sin was that she actually fell in love with her target and it caused her to refuse to work for the Soviet government and she stop giving them British government secrets. The KGB gave her a choice, all though not an easy one in her position. She could leave the country and continue to work for the KGB or they would kill her daughters. She chose the love of her children over the discontent of working for the Soviet Union and the KGB.

The redhead stopped telling her sad story. She then escorted Anna onto the boat. As soon as Anna and the other redhead jumped into the dinghy, the group of assailants from the dancehall caught up to us with their guns, unloading in our direction. We jumped into the boat, fired it up, and chased after the dinghy. At the same time, Jaena noticed that a military transport truck arrived at the Prime Ministers compound with fully loaded soldiers who looked ready to clear the area of any hostile parties.

A little ways down the river, I let most of the people on the boat off at a shallow riverbank. Justin, Jacob, Clarissa, and Ilia got off the boat whiles Jaena insisted she was going to stay and help me chase after Anna and the other redhead. Jaena asked me how I knew both of them and I quickly explained how I have spent most of my career chasing and trying to stop Anna.

I then had to explain to her the harsh reality that was just sinking in. The reality was that my best friend's wife, whom he loves more than anything except his twin daughters, was a KGB agent born into a Soviet KGB family. To this day I still have trouble comprehending, as

some of you also would if you were I, that Amelia
Macradin was a member of the KGB and on Anna Layata's
team.

Jaena and I headed down the Danube River and it
was getting harder to see in the darkening sky. The moon
was out but the passing trees and the cloudy sky were
making the moonlight hard to use. I could barely see
Anna's boat in the distance. Stopping to drop our friends
off cost us a lot of time and ground.

Roughly two miles from where we dropped the
ambassador off and roughly four miles from the ballroom,
we caught up to the dinghy. It was coasting down the
winding river and without its passengers. We had no idea
where they had gone and it was getting colder as the night
went on. We decided to get off at the nearest shallow point
on the riverbank and decided to give a little look for Anna
and Amelia.

We really had no choice, as the boat we were using
was low on fuel. You might be thinking that we had very
little chance to find the two redheads, and you are probably
right. What else was I to do? Did you really think I was
going to give up this close to brining in the Madam? I did
the best I could with the circumstances around me.

After about twenty minutes of looking around the

quiet neighborhood, Jaena and I decided to try to make our way back to our hotel room for we came up with no sign of the girls. They either hid in the water or got lost in this neighborhood. We lost them, mostly because we stopped to drop off the rest of our party. You know we did the right thing because our main job was the protection of the ambassador.

We finally found a cab and ended back at our hotel room where we cleaned up and went to sleep. You would have done the same if you were I and you cannot convince me otherwise. When I got back to my room, it was somewhat quiet because Justin was already sleeping. I was roomed with Justin, Philip and Jacob shared a room, as did Jaena and Clarissa.

I awoke to the sound of knocking on my door at near eight in the morning. The sun was trying to shine through the window as the sound of the wind could be heard whipping against the windowpane. I grabbed the gun that Hungarian officials allowed me to keep only because of the nature of my business within the country. I had to go through extensive questioning and screening before the Hungarian government allowed me to carry a weapon in their country.

I grabbed my gun because I was not going to have

another situation similar to the one in Santa Fe and I sure was not going to wake up caught off guard as I did in Beijing. It was two members of the Hungarian Nemzeti Nyomozó Iroda, translated as the National Bureau of Investigation and joked to be Hungary's equivalent to the FBI.

I thought I was going to have to answer questions regarding the strange death of our team member, Philip Axerdawn. You might think the same thing and if you did, you would be wrong. They were more concerned with the dead couple down the hallway.

According to the police, the couple went to their room to get it on and after taking showers, they were going to get into bed when assailants caught them by surprise. Their room door was broken off its hinges and there was a quick struggle that ensued. The woman, wearing just her lingerie, was battered with her wrists broken and then had her throat slit. Her husband was beaten, probably forced to watch his wife's assault, and then shot in the head. The police started asking me questions because the couple was also American.

Off hand, I had no idea who the couple was and tried to get them to tell me how assailants slid passed all the security in the hotel. The hotel regularly houses delegates from many countries as well as celebrities and high profile individuals. Therefore, the security is top of the line with several guards in the lobby with metal detectors and screenings just to get in the building not to mention guards regularly patrolling each floor.

They insisted that I knew the couple and I asked who the couple was. The officers gave me lip as they told me that they had no clue who the dead couple happened to be. I woke Justin up and after a few minutes, he had the same response as me about not knowing who they were.

I decided, with the officers following me, to head down to Jaena's room to see if she knew who the couple was. I had to walk passed the crime scene to get to her room and what I saw would even make your stomach turn. I could see the woman was lying on her back and it looked as if her head was hanging by one muscle. Covered in blood and distorted from the shot, you could barely make out the face of the man. His face looked like a .44 magnum handgun shot it.

After a moment, I knocked on Jaena's door and after she told us to wait so she could get dressed, she answered the door. I filled her in on what was going on in the room down the hall. We then had a conversation with the two officers similar to the one I had in my room. Even you would be annoyed with the officers because they had the attitude that seemed like everything they said was the truth and we could say nothing but lies.

During our conversation with the officers, I mentioned to Jaena that I found Lucy's red ball and that it was on our boat. You looked confused, so let me explain. Lucy's red ball is a reference to actress Lucille Ball and it is a way to let her know that I saw that one of the crime scene techs was a redhead. The part of the boat was a direct reference to the boat we were in yesterday and the redhead I saw was on a boat as well.

I am not sure about you, but just then, it hit me like a head on car collision. Even though I only got a quick glance at the dead couple, I knew whom they were. After realizing who the redhead was, I had a decently good picture of what went on last night in this hotel.

What I deduced was the following: While Jaena and I rode down the Danube River, Justin and the Malley's went back to our hotel. Justin went to sleep and being a heavy sleeper, he heard nothing. Jacob and Clarissa both got ready for bed and with Clarissa being scared, she stayed in Jacob's room. The Malley's decided to clean up and then relieve one another's stress in an adult fashion when their assailants unexpectedly interrupted, beat, and then assassinated them. While they killed the Malley's, Jaena and I were in some village searching for two women who somehow made it to our hotel before we did.

There were two major reasons that I came to this conclusion. One is that I recognized Clarissa's tattoo running from her wrist up toward her elbow. It is a tattoo of the words 1 Co 13:4-8. It was a reminder for her of the bible verses in 1 Corinthians 13:4-8. The second thing I noticed was the identity of the redhead, even though she wore a baseball cap and tried to cover her face so I would not see her. Amelia Macradin tried to hide from me, but I caught her in the room.

I asked if I could see the bodies and they told me that they had to clear me before they could allow me to do so. I can see that you are thinking just like me; that these two police officers may not be Hungarian Police but Soviet hired guns. It took Jaena a few minutes, but then she had this look on her face as if someone had just turned on several lights in a darkly lit room. She had finally gotten my message about the ball and she understood what my message meant.

I wanted to see if the officers were Hungarian or Soviet hired guns posing as police. This may sound funny to some of you, but I asked one more time if I could see the bodies. Once again, they made it clear that they still considered me a suspect. They mentioned again how they had to clear me before they could let me in the room. That was just what I wanted them to say.

I started to act as if I was mad and I started to rant in Russian. I did not just speak in Russian but I made sure my grammar was out of place and all wrong. If I were speaking in English, it would have sounded like I was a drunken hillbilly from back in the hills who had no formal education. I kept saying this one Russian phrase repeatedly and I kept saying it wrong purposely hoping one officer would get angry and try to correct my grammar.

The taller of the two officers, wearing a plaid jacket, yelled back at me after a minute or two that I should pronounce what I was saying a certain way and not how I was saying it. With his angry and small beady eyes, he told me about his dislike for people like me. I was the kind of person that he thought learned a new language and then tried to act as if I could speak it more fluently than a native speaker could.

It was at this time that the two men tried to escort me out of the room. They had some plan in mind that I was not going to allow to come to fruition. They knew that I had figured out that they were not real police and they began to act accordingly. The tall man, with his Al Capone style hat, pointed his gun at me and motioned for me to leave the room.

Jaena, with the shorter fellow's back to her, put her arms around his neck and began to knock him out. The tall man, hearing his partner choking, turned his head for only a second and it was all I needed. I pushed the gun out of my face and while holding the gun, I kneed him in the stomach. I then twisted the gun and his wrist in such a way that he let go of the gun rather than have his wrist broke.

Immediately, before I could turn the gun on him, the tall man ran his shoulder into me and shoved me out into the hall ramming me into the closed door behind me. The impact forced me to drop the gun and I decided not to try to pick it up. I was going to keep my opponent from grabbing it. Some of you might think that is a stupid idea and that if I shot the man this would end quickly.

Think about it for a moment. What do I get for killing this man? I get no information from him, no idea of the rest of the plans he and his crew may have planned, and it gets me no closer to finding Amelia and Anna. I quickly, and any of you could too, saw that this tall man, roughly 6'5", was all gun strength. What I mean is that he acts tougher and seems like a real bad boy when he is in control and has a gun to back him up. Take away his gun and he is not as tough or as confident as he would like one to think he is.

He charged at me again with, I would assume to be, the intention to put me right through the closed door. He ran at me dropping his shoulder as if he was going to hockey style check me through the door. At this point in my life, being 35, I was still more agile and fit than most of my opponents and it came in hand right here.

I sidestepped the oncoming bull of a man running at me. I am serious, if you picture a bull running at a matador, that is what I saw as the man ran right at me, and I pictured Bugs Bunny making the bull ram into the anvil as this angry fellow crashed into the door. He hit the door with such force that it came crashing down as he knocked it off its hinges. Immediately, I rolled him on his back and began to hit him in the face until he stopped moving.

Not wanting the fight to continue, what was I supposed to do? Some of you look like you have suggestions and at some point I would like to hear them. Anyway, I turned to look around and I saw Jaena dropping the limp knocked out body of the shorter fellow that she had in her hold. Jaena and I hastily ran to the Malley's room to see if Amelia was still there.

She had left the room, probably, as soon as I had locked eyes with here before knocking on Jaena's room. We then ran down to the lobby where laid out on the floor was one of the crime scene tech's that I saw earlier. I bet you are wondering what happened to Justin during all this.

While Jaena and I fought the imposter police, Justin noticed Amelia walking passed his room and followed her to the lobby where the crime scene techs tried to advise him not to continue his pursuit of Amelia. After a quick fistfight, Justin knocked out one crime scene tech and the other fled with Amelia on which Justin gave pursuit to no avail. They got in a black sedan and took off in such a hurry that their car left tire tracks on the road.

After his unsuccessful chase outside the hotel, Justin came in and we called the real police. I am not sure what the assassins' intentions were with knocking on my door. I am neither sure I will ever know nor does it really matter. The police asked us several questions about our knowledge of the assassination of the Malley's.

After spending a few days answering questions about the Malley's and about events at the Prime Ministers ball, the Hungarian police cleared us to leave the country. We arranged for the transfer of the bodies of the Malley's and then we made our way back to the states where we explained what happened in Budapest. Each of us got new assignments after mandatory psych evaluations. For me it was back on the pursuit of Anna Layata.

Queen of the Adriatic

An exterminator is someone paid to remove an infestation or a pest from one's home. They can remove anything from bees, rodents, bats, to mold and other insects. They use pesticides, traps, or glue paper among his methods of removing such pests. In my line of work, an exterminator has a similar job yet the tools and methods are different as well as the type of pest being removed.

In my case, an exterminator's job is to eliminate a person or group of people. This person can be a rogue spy to a political official not "playing ball." When I say the word eliminate, I really mean to kill. Exterminators are assassins or people call them mechanics and their job is to carry out "wet jobs."

Our tools can be anything needed to finish the job. Sniping is a common method used by exterminators. So is poisoning, stabbing, or murder by vehicle. Sniping is the most common method because exterminators can snipe from different heights, angles, or a great distance between the two involved parties.

I spent two years in Vietnam near the end of the war after spending seven months between boot camp and sniper training. I then spent a year training SWAT for the

Baltimore PD. I thought joining the CIA I would be doing a lot more sniping on team missions, but I have not done as much as you think.

Most of my work has been solo and I have already told you the main reason why. For this particular mission, in the spring of Nineteen Eighty-Nine, Aaron Greetox accompanied me. My job was an easy one on paper. I was to exterminate Toby Laine, a rogue spy who was selling secrets and materials to the highest bidders on the black market. He was supposed to infiltrate the Italian black market organization The Little Monk in order to curtail the sale of materials that one may use to build nuclear and or chemical weapons.

Toby is a lean man with a boxer's upper body. He has his dark hair styled as if he were the CEO of his own fortune five hundred company. His Elvis like sideburns cover up his oval shaped jaw.

Not only did Toby fail to do his job, he turned on the CIA and started selling secrets to the highest bidder. Several agents died from the information he sold. Toby always claimed that the CIA had left him for dead in a Middle Eastern prison camp after his capture on an agency mission gone horribly wrong. He spent just over a year in the camp before he escaped. Toby's actions, as he states, are a direct reflection of his time in the camp.

On the particular day that I arrived in Venice, it was very rainy. In mid Nineteen Eighty-Nine, there had been several political unrests in Europe. Among the countries were Germany, Hungary, and Austria. Here in Italy, things were as they had been for years.

This mission to eliminate Toby Laine would be an interesting one for me. Most of the jobs I have done in my career had been solo. To my enemies, I am like a poltergeist. According to them, I bring fear and horror while leaving them wondering what I look like as well as the questioning of if I was actually there. If you have not already noticed, that is how I like to do things and anonymity is usually my friend.

This mission was different. My methods were going to be in check because of the fact that I was to have a spotter assigned to me for this job. The job of a spotter is to watch a sniper's surroundings to make sure he is not compromised or that the enemy does not sneak up behind him as well as provide cover fire if needed. As far as I know, that is there job. The worst part for me was that the spotter assigned to me was my handler Aaron Greetox, with his marine style blond haircut and his drill sergeant demeanor.

Aaron always wears his dark sunglasses and he mostly wears this faded biker jacket. Aaron was running point on this mission and I was just a point and click man brought in to pull a trigger and nothing more. We checked into our hotel and I felt like the walls of an office cubicle were thicker than the ones in our room. It was way too easy to hear our honeymooning neighbors entertaining themselves.

After settling down for a few hours, Aaron and I took a boat drive to the pier where the meeting was supposed to take place. In Venice, the waterways are so prevalent that they have stoplights like our busy streets. We scouted out the area for possible vantage points as well as escape routes for when the job was finished.

I noticed two second-story buildings that each looked like two flat houses. Each had that orange terracotta clay roof associated with Venice old town houses. On one of the second floors, you could see that someone had forgot their laundry was hanging out to dry when it started to rain.

The pier was not that large, and it looked like it was three Ford pickups wide. It could not be any longer than one and a half football fields, and had a wall all along one side with water on the other. At each end of the pier was a wooden staircase allowing entrance to the road above. I decided I would climb to the top of a building at the south end of the pier. From the east was a steep incline from the road above for which a few vehicles could enter to load a day's worth of fish.

There were posts every hundred feet to allow for boat docking. Up on the higher ground above the pier was several boutiques and a busy trattoria serving pastries and small sandwiches. At the end of the street on the north side was a somewhat large produce market selling anything Italian or Mediterranean.

All our information had come from Toby. As far as we knew, Toby was under the impression Aaron was here to take out Modar Hals-Aleaky. Modar was an Iranian who would do anything to wipe his enemies of the planet and to send a message to all who oppose his organizations ideologies. Modar is a world-class whacko and is on the CIA's terrorist watch list.

The actual truth is that Aaron and I were to stop Toby before word gets out that the agency has a rogue agent selling secrets to the highest bidder and that the direct result was the death of American lives. The agency had a man inside Modar's organization and the agency was confident that they could handle Modar as well as find out who gave him his orders. Modar was not the top man, just the public one.

Aaron's job was going to be spotting me and providing me with an escape route. He was going to be letting me know when it is the right time to take the shot and how to avoid detection, which depends on how the meeting is going. I could do all this on my own without a problem, but Aaron insisted I follow his lead. With Aaron outranking me, I had no choice but to comply with his rules. My other option was letting a first time agent take the shot with the possibility of being caught. If the job is to be done, than it shall be done right, and who better to do it and get away with it than a former army ranger sniper.

Aaron, as I found out latter our first night in Venice, was going to be a part of the meeting. Toby was to bring Aaron into the fold as a new member and player within The Little Monk. This meeting was also going to be about the sale of high-powered rifles and enough uranium to make a suitcase sized "dirty" bomb. Information about US agents within the Middle East was also going to be the topic of discussion during this rendezvous.

I bet you can imagine the look on my face as Aaron was telling me that he was to be a part of the meeting and not at my side. It was already bad enough that he was accompanying me on this mission as if he did not trust me to do the job alone. Do you really think I would screw up a mission such as this? With my training, I do not even think that you could screw this up. I guess this was Aaron's compulsive need to be in control.

For Aaron and me it was early to bed and early to rise. I was not supposed to be in Italy for more than a week as the meeting was to take place on the day after we had arrived in the Queen of the Adriatic. The meeting was to take place at midday when traffic and noise were at their height. I arrived an hour early to get up on top of the second story building from which I was to take the fatal shot.

Aaron, meanwhile, took off in a boat to go meet with Toby. He had to make it seem like business as usual for things to work. The pier was uninhabited at the time of Aaron and Toby's arrival. There, however, was already one boat docked and with a few fishing nets in the back, it looked as if the owners would soon be back. As Toby set up a test fire dummy, it started to rain. Toby wore blue jeans and a business casual dark long sleeved shirt with the cuffs rolled up to his elbows.

I thought Toby was going to spot me as he set up the dummy near the building that I was perched up on. At approximately two in the afternoon local time, a small-unmarked black vehicle came down the ramp to the southern end of the pier. Things were going to get really ugly real soon. I equipped my silencer and waited for Aaron to give me the signal. My brown hair and my short-sleeved green shirt was getting soaked as the rain began to get heavier.

I unbuttoned my green shirt, laying on my wet white undershirt, while readying myself for the shot. I adjusted the scope as I tried to keep the lens dry from the heaving rain. I can see that you are wondering when I was going to get my surprise of the day. It seems that I get one every mission. I got the biggest surprise when the black van parked at the far north end of the pier and three men pulled out.

The first man had on a navy blue dress shirt and tuxedo style pants with a brown belt. He had a huge golden belt buckle and a haircut no longer than Aaron did. With his brown dress shoes, he walked as if he owned the place and that he wanted to get this over with quickly. I recognized him as Iranian Modar Hals-Aleaky.

The second man pulled his sunglasses off his dark hair and over his eyes. He had on a long black trench coat covering his jeans and a dark shirt. He looked like he was Modar's personal bodyguard. You would think the same if you saw the two of them standing together, partly because their skin tone was the same and partly because his body looked defensive when Toby went to shake hands with Modar.

The third man got out of the vehicle and for a second or two my body froze at the sight of the man I saw standing there. He was a dark blonde wearing thin framed dark shades. He had on a dark jacket one would expect a fighter pilot to wear. When he lowered his glasses for just moment, I knew what I was going to do. I had to keep this third man from harm. You would do the same for your best friend and you cannot deny it. Daniel Macradin walked out of the vehicle and as I saw him get out, Aaron caught a glimpse of the look on my face. It was one of familiarity but surprise.

After about twenty minutes of them all talking, my body was getting restless. I saw Toby hand Modar a large envelope, which he handed to the man in the trench coat. I thought that there was at least three spots that would have been the perfect time to take Toby out, as that was the mission, but Aaron never gave me a signal to take the shot.

Finally, after what felt like hours, Toby grabbed a high-powered rifle and gave it to Modar. Modar began inspecting it and I could see him asking several questions.

Periodically, I could see Aaron glancing up at me, and he had this look as if he knew something was about to happen and he was not going to tell me. I had half a mind to shoot both Toby and Modar followed by me high tailing it out of the area while running across the rooftops. You would too if you were me or in my situation.

Daniel moved the test dummy down to the north end of the pier and placed it next to the vehicle. Modar and his bodyguard walked over and stood next to Aaron positioning themselves between Toby and the boats. I glanced at Aaron, but again he gave me no signal. I saw something in Aaron's hand but I could not make out what it was he had. He hid it just out of my full view.

I took a quick look at Daniel, and I saw something that I am not sure I was supposed to see. For just a second or two I could see a red dot from a laser beam on Daniel's chest. It got me to start scanning rooftops and the surrounding area for another possible shooter. At this time, I could see Toby was backing up to the point that he was out of my view.

Soon as Toby was out of my view, I heard a gunshot and assumed he was just test firing the gun for Modar to see the impact it would cause. Not five seconds later my heart skipped several beats as I saw Daniel drop to his knees as a river of his own blood began to cover the pier. SON OF A…! I grabbed my rifle and jumped down from the second story to the first floor rooftop below. As I hit, pieces of terracotta shingles slid down the roof and onto the pier below.

I did not care what Aaron's orders were. I was going to put several bullets into Toby's body and maybe one or two in Modar's head. As I started to search for Toby, I caught a glimpse of Aaron grabbing Modar and his bodyguard as they entered the boat and began to take off. I fired a few shots at the boat, but none of them hit anyone. I did put a shot or two into the back of the boat. I was not sure if I put a hole in the tank but I was hopeful. What would you do if you were I and just saw your best friend gun down?

After firing at the boat, I had to reload my rifle, which only carried ten shots. Normally I have better accuracy than I had just a minute ago. I caught sight of Toby jogging toward the top of the ramp, so I ran across the rooftop to cut him off at street level. He turned his rifle toward me and began to fire at my feet.

With pieces of the orange roof shattering from every bullet hit, I stopped in my tracks and began running back in the direction I had come. My options were limited and this was the best one available. You would do the same with such limited choices. I was fortunate to stay just a step ahead of the trail of shots fired at me.

Toby's gun went click. He ran out of ammunition and had to reload. I took this opportunity to hop onto a pile of crates that someone staked against the building. Next, I jumped onto the pier. I picked myself up and switched weapons. I dropped my heavy sniper rifle for my Beretta M9 pistol. As I did, Toby fired a pistol shot narrowly missing my head.

He then turned and ran down the pier and tried to jumpstart the vehicle that Modar left behind. At this point, both you and I can assume that Aaron is coming up with some bogus story to keep his cover in tacked as well as explaining why Toby killed Daniel. With my heart pounding, I knelt on one knee and peppered the rear driver-side tire. It shows in your face that you can see why I blew out the tire.

Toby took another shot at me and once again, he missed. With his accuracy, even you could see, he was never going to win a sharp shooting medal. His shot gave him enough time to get out of the vehicle and he headed toward the stairs at the northern edge of the pier. I got up, in pursuit, and ran to the other end of the pier.

Trying to catch up to Toby, I did a Jackie Chan style stunt by jumping off the wall of the half story high street, then jumping off the van, and onto the street itself. I continued my chase after Toby, who was now running into a crowd of shoppers and people eating a late lunch.

Next, Toby did what anyone in this type of situation might do, and you see it a lot in movies. He fired a gunshot into the air, sending most of the people running and screaming. Toby thought he would ditch me by ducking into the trattoria and running out the back. Unlucky for him, I saw where he ran and followed him into the trattoria.

Toby noticed that I had entered the trattoria and he headed to the kitchen in the back as he shoved two small round tables in my path in hopes to slow me down. I jumped over both and maintained my pursuit toward the kitchen. Toby noticed me enter and began knocking pastry trays off the racks that they were sitting. When that failed to create the distance Toby had wanted, he grabbed hold of an attractive young brunette. He used her to shield himself as he backed out of the trattoria and into the alley.

I slammed the back door of the trattoria against the side of the building and could see Toby throw the woman hard against a metal garbage can. The alley was very small, just wide enough to allow one moped to enter. At one end, it led to an area of old seventeenth century homes and flats. At the other end, it opened to a town plaza with a circular fountain children love to throw coins into and make wishes. The plaza is large with several boutiques and restaurants of all sizes.

I stopped to check the woman and see if she was all right. When she shook me off, I continued to chase after Toby, but the momentary stop to check the woman caused me to lose sight of where he had gone. I found a sports jacket lying on the ground where Toby had shed it. As not to spook the people in the plaza, I holstered my pistol and then buttoned up my green shirt as I walked toward the fountain looking for Toby, who could not have gotten that far away from me.

I looked around the plaza and in the pouring rain, I could not see as well as I would have liked. Even you would have had problems in the rain. It was hard enough that you would have needed to have your windshield wipers on full speed if you were driving in this rain. With my adrenaline flowing, all the buildings with their beige or white exterior color made the people blend in to the point that they looked the same.

For a moment, with the sound of the fountain water

flowing, I had tunnel vision and could only focus on what was in front of me. Quickly, I shook that off and began to focus on everything around me. You would too with my training and with what just happened. I noticed a somewhat tall man walking a little faster than the normal flow of the people in the plaza, so I slowly walked around the fountain and toward him.

I did not see the man turn around to look at me but I could see him looking into the window of one shop. I assume he used the window as a mirror to see what was behind him. The next thing I noticed is that he knocked an older woman to the ground and started running down the side street toward a nearby canal. I could tell it was Toby when he turned and took another shot at me. I guess you and I will never know how the agency put Toby into the field with his inaccuracy because this shot also missed me.

Toby took off over a canal bridge and I did the same. When he crossed, Toby started running along a small walkway between beige buildings and a stream of water with boats passing by. Not seeing many people, I pulled out me pistol and continued after Toby. We ran for about a quarter mile until there was a big enough opening that it looked like Toby had no were to run.

He looked back at me, backed up a few steps, and

started to run as if he was going to try to jump across the gap between the two walkways even though there was a sizable amount of water in his way. Even you can see things were not looking well for Toby. I think you would still do the same if you were in Toby's shoes. It was either Toby's lucky or my unlucky day because when Toby jumped, he landed on the back end of a slow moving gondola.

When he stood up, I took my first gunshot catching him flush in the right shoulder. My second shot missed him as he tumbled across the gondola, rocking it and scaring the gondolier. By the time I had aimed for my third shot, Toby had already floated far enough down the canal that it was not worth shooting. By looking around, I can see that most of you would have had either panic or anger if you were I in this situation. It would have depended on if you were feeling anxiety about not putting him down and facing the repercussions from the agency or if you were disgusted that Toby got away.

I ran back to the canal bridge where I had seen a small two-seater motor boat tied to a post. I got into the boat and had to hotwire the engine to get it running. After doing so, I drove the boat straight for the intersection and head toward the gondola that Toby was riding. The gondolier was not that fast with his paddle because I caught up to them more easily than I should have.

Toby had his gun pointed at the gondolier in hopes that it would scare me into backing away so he would not kill the man. Some of you look like you would back off and you know who you are. I decided not to slow the boat down and Toby made his second best shot of the day. He put a bullet into the front of the boat I was driving, and I could see smoke pouring out of the hole.

I pushed the engine to go as fast as it could while turning the boat toward the gondola. Right in the intersection of two waterways, I split the gondola as I ran right through it with the boat I was driving. You probably would have felt sorry for the gondolier just as I had. Taking people on ride all across the city may have been his source of income, and I just took that from him. It is what I had to do and you know it.

Toby looked as if his shoulder was screaming in pain as the boat quickly sank. He tried to swim away, but with a bullet in his right shoulder, he could not get very far. I pulled the boat close to a canal bridge and jumped holding on to the side of the bridge as I started climbing up. The boat I was driving slowly floated down the canal as I turned to see Toby swimming to solid ground.

Soon as he stood up, I put two rounds into his chest. His body hit the ground as I ran over and approached him. It only took me seconds to get to his body, but by then he was already dead. I took his belt buckle, which had the seal of The Little Monk on it, as proof that the job was complete.

I headed back to the hotel to see if Aaron was there. Not seeing him in our room and not knowing where he was, I decided to take a shower and then start to read my wife's newest book. As the sun started to go down, I still had not heard or seen from Aaron, so I went to a nearby restaurant where I ordered a club sandwich, a manicotti, and a glass of Italian vermouth.

I must have fallen asleep shortly after I got back to my room because when I woke up the sun was up with no rain, the birds were out, and it was six a.m. I still had not seen Aaron since Toby shot Daniel. I looked around the room to see if his belongings were still here but I could not find anything that belonged to Aaron. I was feeling a little angry and betrayed at this moment. In my shoes, I think you would have felt the same way.

When the time came, I took a taxi to the airport. With the plane ticket already purchased, what else was I supposed to do? I went to the counter to check in. I was to check in as if I was going to be the flights air marshal back to the States. Things got worse for me when the lady at the counter told me that I had a flagged passport and I could not leave the country. I leaned over the counter, and with her blue eyes, she gave me this evil stare as if I was her child and had just broke the living room lamp.

I got a quick look at a memo on her desk. It had my picture on it as well as a note to call Interpol and Italian authorities if anyone spotted me trying to leave the country. She leaned her head back and brushed her dark hair out of her eyes as she grabbed a phone to call airport security. I grabbed my passport of the counter, picked up my bag, and then I hightailed toward the front exit.

Two chubby looking guards tried to block my path out of the crowded airport. They said something in Italian, but I did not understand a word they said. One guard reached for his weapon and I reacted by hitting him just below the Adam's apple with the palm of my hand. He started coughing as he fell to his butt. The second guard grabbed me from behind and then put me in a headlock.

I hit him in the gut with my elbow, and momentarily he let go of the hold. He stepped to the side of me and then reapplied his hold thinking he would hold me there as he repeatedly hit me in the face. Quickly, I threw my arm around his head and clasped it with my other hand under his chin. I followed that by swiftly pulling and throwing his body over my leg. When he hit the ground and let go of his hold, I gave him a punch to the sternum.

I then grabbed my bag and exited the airport. I got in the first cab that came to a stop at the curb and had the driver take me to the train station. I walked into the huge station with a large lobby. In the center was several benches for people waiting for a train to leave. The station reminded me of Union Station in Chicago.

I walked over to the ticket window and waited in line. The old fellow at the counter asked me where I wanted to go. I asked for a ticket to Innsbruck, Austria. I gave him my Russian passport. The way I figured if I could not get out of the country as me, than Romani Gudenchki was going to try to leave.

The fellow at the counter gave me a ticket and told me to board at track four. The trip was going to be at least a day as we went through the mountains. I boarded the train with no one trying to stop me. Two suspicious men boarded just after I had gotten on the train.

I dropped my bag off in my room, which was very small. It was only big enough for a bed and a closet and that was all that I had needed. I went to the dining car to grab breakfast, and the taller of the two suspicious men followed right behind me. After I sat down and ordered my food, the tall man, who looked a little like Jaws from the James Bond films, slid over and sat next to me.

He jammed a gun into my ribs and started to tell me about how I had to get up and follow him. I made mention of him removing the gun before he had a broken face, but he shook me off. He had big marble sized green eyes that looked mad as he told me I was under arrest because, as a member of Italian authorities, he was bringing me in at the next stop.

I wanted to see police identification but as I asked, he shoved the gun deeper into my ribs. Even you would be suspicious of this man based on his actions. I could hear the hammer of the gun click as he waited for me to get up. I used my agility and forcefully slammed the man's head into the table we sat at. I must have broken his nose because he was profusely bleeding down his face. I then hit him with my palm across his lower chin and sent him to the floor, sleeping like a baby. I assured everyone in the car that everything was fine and that he was still hung over from too much drinking.

I took the man out of the dining car and acted as if I would take him back to his room when I really opened the door of one of the room cars and dumped him off the train. I then went back to the dining car, took my food, and went back to my room. Things were quiet for a few hours until I heard a fight and struggle outside my door. After the fight ended, a knocking on my door followed it.

With my record of noises outside my hotel room doors, you can see why I was reluctant to open my door. You would be too if you have had my experiences. Since the knocking persisted and was getting louder, I decided against my better judgment and answered the door. It was one of the train conductors asking me if I had seen a tall fellow wearing a suit with no tie and brown suspenders. I lied to the man by telling him I had not seen the man since I grabbed my food and came back to my room. He wanted to know if I saw the man recently because his friend was looking for him.

Reality check, something fishy was going on and the two men that followed me on to the train were right in the middle of it all. Not five minutes later, there was another knock at my door and I answered it to a robust man with a large beard and hands the size of basketballs. He hit me hard in the face, and then closed my door behind him as he pointed a gun at me. Sadly, my Beretta was in my bag in the closet.

This robust man also gave me the same story about us getting off at the first stop past the mountains of the Alps. This was the second time I had heard this song and it was even more ridiculous coming from this stout man. I am not sure what would be going through your mind at this point, but I was already formulating a plan on how to get rid of the nuisance standing in front of me.

We could feel the train slowing down and we were not sure why. We found out later that there had been a slight rockslide and that several huge boulders covered the tracks up ahead. Since the train had stopped, the man motioned for me to get up and walk with him off the train. The man also instructed me not to resist or make a scene. In all this, he tried to order me to tell him what I had done to his partner, but I kept quiet and said nothing. I was going to keep completely quiet as I could see that not answering his questions only angered him more.

We walked off the train and headed toward the bushy hills a mile or two away. The area was just outside the tunnel dug into the side of the Alps heading towards Austria. It was a hot and sunny midday as we took our walk. It was a hilly countryside and reminded me of the hillside seen in the movie The Sound of Music.

This guy with the gun only made two mistakes and

it cost him. He was squinting in the bright sunlight as we walked toward the hills and away from the train. Mistake number one came when he told a conductor, as we left the train, that he was with Italian authorities and turned his head to look at the conductor standing on the edge of the train.

His second mistake happened earlier when he stood in my room. The way he dressed was the biggest clue to whom he was and what he was doing on the train. He wore the same belt buckle that I had taken off Toby's body. I am not sure how those in the Little Monk knew where I was or even what I had done. You can try to come up with any reason and it would be as good of a guess as any guess I would give you.

As he turned his head, I spun around and dropped to my knees. I hit the man in his groin twice and you could see the pain in his face. I then rose to my feet and used my left hand to shove the gun straight into the air as he fired one shot toward the clouds. I continued to hit him hard in his bicep and then I tossed him over my shoulder to the ground. I twisted the gun fast enough out of his hand that his trigger finger broke as it bent backwards.

Some of the riders saw this fight ensue, so I assured them that the situation was under control. I convinced them that the man was trying to rob me and threatened to kill me. They completely bought that story. I took the pistol apart and left the clip and slide of the gun on the ground and took the rest with me onto the train as I went back to my room.

The rest of the train ride went without a hitch. I enjoyed the peace and quiet of the train as we entered Austria. I was lucky enough to catch a flight from Innsbruck to D.C. The next morning when I went to work, you can imagine the surprise as well as anger when I noticed Aaron's car in the Agency parking lot and found out that he was doing paperwork in his office. Later that day I had a meeting with Aaron's boss to discuss my mission in Italy as well as a few other things. It was not until I left for lunch an hour later that life threw me a curveball and I was determined to hit it out of the stadium.

News Capital of the World

The courtroom was packed full of people waiting to catch a glimpse of what it was like to work for the CIA. The jury was full of twelve people who could not be more different in age, race, jobs, and cultural background. The District Attorney decided to take on this case. He was an overworked and overtired looking individual. He wore dark blue suits that looked like he paid more than most people make in a month just for one of them. He wore a blue tie with small yellow squares that look as if they are spinning when you look at them, and it probably cost him the same as some people spend monthly on their car payment.

He is a slightly balding individual who is tall enough to dunk a basketball but is not athletic enough to do so. He had that older man slightly pudgy face sitting under his salt and pepper hair. His opponent was a chubby dark skinned bald man who looked as if he and his client had no reason to be in the courtroom. He looked as if he enjoyed one too many baked goods.

Now the District Attorney looked at me and began to speak, "over the past few days we have sat and listened to you describe in detail your missions on trying to catch the 'Madam' Anna Layata. Now may I ask what that has to do with the defendant and his crimes against the Agency and his country?"

I took a moment of silence and then I looked him dead in the eyes as I gave him my answer. "Everything I have told you, every mission, and every trial I have gone through is because of that man sitting in the defendant's chair."

I took a drink of water and continued to speak. "Let me explain what he has actually done to me. First, our defendant went to Mexico in late 1980 on the trail of a Soviet ring smuggling materials into the US to make nuclear weapons. He chased a spy by the name of Anna Layata. One of her teammates was hunting her because he wanted to take control of her team and he hated being on a team lead by a woman. He tried to kill her and our defendant was mistaken for one of her new cohorts. He had the local cartel put out a hit on both of them. They ended up in a broken rundown shack sharing body heat to keep warm, and from what I have learned, they eloped in the summer of 1981."

"In 1982, the defendant knew that sending me to Santa Fe would send me right into the hands of a small team sent by the Madam. He thought they would kill me and he told them to screw with my mind first. That is why I ended up in the desert, but I survived and it angered," pointing to the defendant I finished my thought "him to no end. He orchestrated the capture of the Flauntain's knowing that if he sent me, I would find The Chosen Ones compound. He was the one who told Anna that I was in Jordan and she informed Ominia of whom I really was."

Continuing to describe what the defendant has done, I looked intently at juror number six. "Our defendant was the handler of Adam Karzikowski, so he knew what I was getting into in Amsterdam. He figured his wife and her friends would dispose of me but a British agent named Daniel Macradin made sure that would not happen. That was the last time most of those 'conference members' were heard from. He knew Aziha Moniva was working with some Triad members and Chinese officials in interrogating Kwai Xui. His wife had sent her to do just that."

"So what does the defendant decide to do? He sends me to extract Kwai hoping Aziha and the Triad would put me in an early grave. Aziha had to live through a broken back thanks to me as well as an eighth of the Triad being disposed. Next, I had to watch as an associate of Anna Layata tried to kill my wife, and our defendant was the reason Pavel Korinniko and Dingus McFaddin knew where I was. Anna even has my friend's wife pulled out of a multi-year operation because she refused to play ball."

"He is the one who left me in a Soviet prison for nine months after he called his wife to stop me from doing anything to her family. He did it because he was enraged that I angered Wilhelm Shlekneil enough that he ordered a hit and had Pavel's body dumped in the Black Forest Mountains. He is also the reason that Anna Layata and an execution squad caused so much trouble and destruction in Budapest. They tried to have me killed but THEY FAILED! I FIGURED they would have learned NOT TO TRY TO KILL ME! It never goes well for those who try."

The District Attorney Steven Owning walked toward the stand and proceeded to ask me a few more questions. "Is it true that the defendant ordered the hit of your friend Daniel Macradin and then left you high and dry in Italy?"

"Yes, Steven, it is. He may have thought that by doing so in front of me, I would not be able to carry out my mission and eliminate his associate Toby Laine. He may have thought it torture for me to see my friend shot in front of me. Either way, he puts me on the Italian no fly list and tried to have authorities detain me from leaving the country. He put his associates at the train stop just in case I tried to leave by rail if I had escaped capture. When he found out I made it back to the States, he ordered a hit be put out on my head and if not for Lester Penada, the defendant's boss, intercepting a package I would be dead."

"Joey," asked Steven in a calm voice "why does the defendant hate you so much he wants to kill you?" At this point, the defendant was looking rather squeamish in his cheap suit and short hairstyle.

"Why does he hate me? That is an easy answer. He hates the fact that for seven years he held the highest marks, the fastest times, and was the best agent ever to come out of the Farm. Agents training for fieldwork looked to our defendant as a model of what an agent leaving the Farm should look like. I shattered every record at the Farm that he had, and he DESPISED ME because he was no longer the best. He also hated the fact that one screw up which got an asset killed in the field ended his career as an agent. The CIA gave him the choice to become a handler or work in Columbia indefinitely. He chose the path that gave him more freedom to travel so he could see his wife."

"The fact is, after all the incidents I have caused, I have not been taken out of the field. It is because of that that the defendant despises me. He HATES the fact that I get to stay as a field agent and they pulled him all the while feeling that what I have done is worse than what he accidentally did. There is also the fact that I have tried to put his wife, Anna Layata, out of commission ever since she tried to have me killed in Cambodia back in 1975."

Looking at the defendant, you can easily see why he looks so uncomfortable and squeamish. It did not help him that the one person on the planet he wished he would never see again was not only not dead but causing his world to crumble all around him.

I want everyone to understand what I had done to cause his world to crumble. Therefore, I explained it to the jury. I am talking about his organization that he and Anna had built.

"The reason our defendant looked so scared but also surprised on the first day when I walked in here was the fact that I was supposed to be dead. I went completely dark after getting back from Italy in 1989 and I stayed that way until two months ago. It had been seven years and one month since the world thought I had died when I came back to the living. He and his wife built an organization that fifty-five of the world's top countries, the US and Russia included, did not even know existed. They had politicians, government agents, warlords, kingpins, and anyone you can name working for or with them."

"Most countries had problems with organized crime

groups or spy rings, and they thought they knew the group's leaders. The truth is that whom they thought was the leaders really had four to five people in power over them who were still under the authority of Anna and our defendant. All the political corruption you have heard about over the last few years taking place from Guatemala to Brazil is because I SHED A LIGHT UPON IT! The warlord whose body was found with no head is because I SENT IT TO HIS BROTHER!"

"The military leader of Turkey who has not been seen since 1990 can be blamed on me. Not even his brother knows what happened to him. I know where his body is and I had better know because I PUT HIM THERE! That is right, Aaron. He was on YOUR PAYROLL and I put him in his grave. Like everything else that has happened to you and your wife since late Nineteen Eighty-Nine, you can blame ME. I BURIED HIS ORGANIZATION, JUST LIKE I SAID I WOULD!"

Right then the judge hit his gavel on the bench and called for a recess and that we were going to reconvene tomorrow in the early morning. As I got off the stand and walked passed the defendant, Aaron Greetox, I let him know exactly what I thought. He looked as if he was having a never-ending nightmare.

"Aaron, you may have been thinking that you were doing the right thing when you and Anna eloped. I told you she was the Devil incarnate and you have sold your soul to her. Now I am just an agent of God brining you your punishment for the sins you have committed. I am NOT TO BLAME for this happening to you! You BROUGHT THIS on yourself, NOT me. You might think that the last seven years have been hell with everything falling apart around you. Well, Aaron, welcome to hell and I have been your tour guide!"

Five days later, I went to visit Aaron in a FBI holding cell nearby the court house. He was waiting to step onto the stand to speak to the jury. Aaron wanted nothing to do with the witness stand but his lawyer insisted he takes the stand. They were trying to use some mental defense saying that he was not responsible because he was mentally unstable and unable to control his emotional stat around Anna and that she brainwashed him to do the things he was on trial for doing. I could, and even you could, see right through that crap defense and I know that he made most of those choices on his own.

I met Aaron in some interrogation room with dim lights and a two-way mirror. He could not move much cuffed to the floor all the while wearing the trademark prison orange jumpsuit. His lawyer looked very unhappy to see me and looked as if I had no business being in the room. I sat down at the table across from Aaron and put a folder with the morning news on the table. I waited for Aaron to speak first.

"Joey, what is this all about? Have you not caused me enough pain and suffering? What can you possibly have left to say to me?"

I took a good long look at him and then I quietly asked him, "Have you read this morning's paper?"

"NO! What the hell does that have to do with anything anyway?"

I threw the Washington Post World News section on the table. I pushed my chair a little back from the table and waited for Aaron to pick up the paper. He looked at the front-page photo and looked back at me with a little confusion in his face. The headline read, "Several attacks on Serbian security in Kosovo including a hotel explosion." The aftermath of the explosion was on the front page.

The article talked about the explosion and about the number of people who died in the blast. On page three of the paper, the story continued and it is there where Aaron started realizing the true nature of what I was capable of going to in order to stop his organization and holding him accountable for his actions.

The paper showed the faces of two children. The girl was age ten and the boy seven. The paper did not give the children's age but Aaron knew that was how old they were. Aaron took one look at the pictures of the two faces. Then he threw the paper against the wall and buried his face in his hands. He had the most horrific look of sadness on his face that anyone could possibly have. The look on his face was the exact look you would expect from someone who just found out the news he had.

Next, I opened the folder and I took out three blown up pictures. I placed them down on the table in front of Aaron. I let him examine the pictures and I watched as reality set into his body. For a moment, he stopped breathing. His lawyer had a look of bewilderment, and it is because I do not think he knew exactly what the content was of what I placed in front of Aaron. After minutes of looking at the pictures, Aaron leaned over his chair and began to puke.

Very calmly, I looked at Aaron as I gathered the pictures and stood up from my chair. I opened the door and just before I left, I turned back to Aaron and spoke with conviction.

"Our time is done. Your tour is over. Hope you have enjoyed the ride."

Six hours later, guards were responding to a ruckus in cellblock B of the nearby prison. Some of the inmates were shouting and when the guards responded, the scene shocked them. Aaron was hanging from a bed sheet tied to the rafter on the ceiling of his cell. The coroner pronounced Aaron dead on the scene by strangulation due to suicidal hanging.

Now let me explain what happened in Kosovo. Let me shed some light on the bombing of the hotel and the three photos that I had showed Aaron. I was not responsible for the attacks on Serbian security but I was the reason for the bombing and the pictures Aaron had seen before I left.

I left the courtroom after being on the stand and I went back to my hotel room. I could not go home because Athena was not speaking to me. She knew that I was going dark and we communicated over the years as best we could. I saw her and the kids only a couple times when I had snuck into countries where she had taken our children because of her work. About three years into this mission my wife and I divorced because she could not take not knowing where I was or if I was safe and she could not put our children through this. She told the kids that I had ran off, that I was never coming back, and I have not seen them since.

Late in the evening on that day, I received a call from Lester Penada. Lester was Aaron's superior and was my CIA contact whiles I was dark. He kept a false account that only he knew of, open with funds so I could survive. It was not much but enough for me to survive and continue my mission. There were times when I took money from members of Anna and Aaron's organization and deposited it into this account that Lester and I had access to.

He called me to let me know that there was credible intelligence on a high-ranking member of the Madam's organization. We had a solid lead from British MI6 that a meeting was going to be taking place in the Kosovo city of Pristina. I took a CIA jet and was there just after lunch that next morning.

The intelligence provided had several pictures of the target entering and exiting a hotel room at the northern edge of town. The town looked like any other post-Soviet city. It was booming but not as much as other former Soviet cities. Our target, a former KGB Spy, had two children with them when spotted at the hotel.

Through contacts that I had made, I spent a full day

setting up a meeting with the target. Finally, after a day and a half I had a meeting with the target. The target thought that I was looking for a way to sell weapons and materials. The target was convinced they were meeting a former Ukrainian major who served the Soviet Union faithfully.

I used my ninja like skills that I had developed over the last few years. I had become something like the fictional character Jason Bourne in that I can get in and out of a place and make it seem as if I was never there to begin with. I noticed that the target was staying on a second floor hotel room with two children.

I went to the local market and purchased some cooking items. I bought sugar, milk and eggs. I did not need the milk but bought it to make it seem as if I was going to be baking something. I had brought in two empty bottles of soda that I had filled partially with butane. I already had a bag of nails, small metal scraps, and pins.

I waited till our target left the room for a meeting with an associate. I knew the target would not be back for a few hours because the target and I were going to be meeting within two hours. I set everything up right before I left. In a little time, things were going to happen. I waited outside the hotel until I saw the target coming down the road. We were going to be meeting at a café just blocks from the hotel, and the target was told that the person they were meeting was a paranoid individual thinking people were out to get him.

The CIA had lent me a small box containing actual materials that could be used for a dirty bomb. It was mostly for show to try to convince the target that I had more to sell given enough time to move the materials. We met at lunch time and by then I had already set up everything outside the targets hotel room where a bodyguard was watching over the two children staying in the room.

We sat outside on one table located on the side of the building. The sun was hot with not a cloud in the sky. The city skyline could be seen behind where the target was sitting. Behind her was a row of bushes covering the side of the road heading back toward the hotel that the target was staying at. She wore her auburn hair in a ponytail and had on a thin pair of baby blue tinted sunglasses. She wore light brown shorts with a tight white tank top and an unbuttoned cream colored short sleeved blouse.

The woman's eye could be seen through the tint of the thin rimmed glasses and she looked as if she had somewhere she would have rather been. We began talking about me, and why I wanted to unload my materials. I gave her a story about needing money to hide from some people that I had double crossed. The target could care less about my story, and I could tell she just wanted to see what I had and if it was worth the price of business.

I put the small box on the table and she opened it, examining the contents. She took out a small object and used it to measure how radioactive the material actually was. It was at that moment that a large explosion could be heard nearby and smoke could be seen in the near distance. The noise knocked the target out of her chair. After the initial blast ended, the target got up and noticed from what direction the explosion happened. She got up, apologized that she had to leave, and asked if I could meet her in forty-eight hours at this same place to continue this deal.

I figured that she knew where that blast came from or she had a good idea of where it happened. It was at that moment I pulled out my pistol, pointed it at her, and demanded that she stay seated.

"Where do you think you are going, Mrs. Layata?"

She had a scared look on her face and spoke with a timorous tone. She looked as if multiple thoughts were running rampant in her brain as she tried to answer my question.

"That blast. I have to go. I have got this thing with my children that I promised I would take them to and I need to see if they are ready. Sorry."

"You are going nowhere Anna. Sit right back down. Plus, I do not think your children made it out of that explosion."

"How could you know that? How could you possibly say something likes that?"

"How, Anna? I do not think you realize WHO I AM!"

We got up and took a ride in her car to the place of the blast. She got out of the car and started to break down as she saw the destruction of the two MacGyver style bombs I had unleashed. One bomb was placed near her room and the other was near the boiler for maximum damage.

"I told you they did not make it."

"How could you do this?" Anna screamed in an angry voice. "Michael Hansgrove, is what you call yourself? How could you? Before today I had never met you and I have no idea who you think you are but you will PAY for THIS! You can believe me on that promise."

"Anna, you really have no clue who I am. If you did, you would not be making these threats that we both know you cannot carry out. Half your organization is gone and the other half does not trust you anymore. Your husband is on trial for treason to his country and you just lost your kids. Thanks, by the way."

"YOU PIECE OF SH..! I AM GOING TO KILL YOU! You just signed your death warrant and I WILL COLLECT."

"Anna, you do not scare me but you should fear me. You brought this on yourself. You NEVER should have tried to kill me."

"Kill you, Michael. I have never met you, so how could I have tried to kill you?"

I looked right into her hazel eyes as I unzipped my leather jacket. "What about Phnom Penh in 1975? Does that ring a bell to you?"

She answered, "I was there and I left a few Americans for the wolves to feast on."

"You tried to kill me then and you FAILED! You then tried to have Ominia Romitti a Kulo Kula do the job for you. His organization tried to assassinate me but we know what really happened to Ominia and his boys when the FAILED! Aziha Moniva, do you remember her and what happened when you had her try to kill me? She took a few shots at me but in the end, she too FAILED! Both of the Korinniko brothers, on your orders, tried to put me in a grave and they FAILED! One of your biggest mistakes was having Pavel shoot my wife."

I took a step back from Anna, and I continued to speak all the while watching her brain try to make sense of what I was saying.

"You probably forgot about Lubyanka prison. You had your chance then. Same happened with your try at a ballroom on the Danube River. Both of those times you FAILED!"

Anna looked at me, and with conviction now in her voice she yelled back at me, "Those events might have been true if not for the fact that the man they happened to was assassinated by a man hired by my husband. In the end I won."

"In Lubyanka prison, Anna, you told me that this game of chess we were playing was over and that you were taking my king. When your husband hired the Iceman, you believed you had my king and only because I LET YOU."

With my right hand I started tearing at the Hollywood monster style makeup covering my lower face. I then took off the mask tailored to my face made by the finest tech boys of the CIA. It was a mask made to allow the wearer to assume the role or identity of another person and it is made in a way that is very hard to tell it is not real skin. I also stopped disguising my voice that had been sounding like it had an Athenian accent.

I grabbed an unused handkerchief out of my coat pocket and wiped my face, removing the last remnants of the makeup. Raising the gun at her, I continued to speak.

"I intercepted your husband's message to the Iceman, killed him myself, and then I staged my own death. For the past seven years, everything that has happened to you, your husband, or your organization was because I CAUSED IT! You know damn well who I am. My name is Joseph Scapeotto!"

"This is not possible! You are supposed to be dead. My husband confirmed it with pictures."

"He confirmed it, Anna because I let him. Now, if you are going to put a king in check, you need to make sure you can finish the game. For you, Anna Layata, this is CHECKMATE!"

With that being said, you could hear the sound of a gunshot going off. It was shortly thereafter, followed by the sound of a camera taking three pictures. I told you how this mission began and with no time to kill, now you understand why I took the actions that I did. With that in mind, case closed, mission accomplished.